DARK JUSTICE

A GIA SANTELLA CRIME THRILLER
BOOK 13

KRISTI BELCAMINO

LIQUID MIND PUBLISHING

Copyright © 2021 by Kristi Belcamino. All rights reserved. No part of this publication may be copied, reproduced in any format, by any means, electronic or otherwise, without prior consent from the copyright owner and publisher of this book.

Liquid Mind Publishing
This is a work of fiction. All characters, names, places and events are the product of the author's imagination or used fictitiously.

GIA SANTELLA CRIME THRILLER SERIES

Enjoying the Gia Santella series? Scan below to order more books today!

Vendetta

Vigilante

Vengeance

Black Widow

Day of the Dead

Border Line

Night Fall

Stone Cold

Cold as Death

Cold Blooded

Dark Shadows

Dark Vengeance

Dark Justice

Deadly Justice

Deadly Lies

PROLOGUE

I WAS DYING FOR A CIGARETTE.

But the senator standing before me in his tuxedo droned on about his pancreatitis and how he could only drink top shelf bourbon or he'd end up in the hospital or something.

Yawn.

I tried not to be obvious as I glanced over his shoulder at the rest of the chandelier-lit room. The backdrop on four sides was the San Francisco skyline at night—one of my favorite views in the world.

Although the music at the gala was low and sultry, the clink of Champagne glasses and rustle of silk and taffeta and the murmur of drunken voices made it difficult for me to hear what the senator was saying.

And that was just fine by me.

I was sort of zoning out, thinking that maybe instead of a cigarette I could rustle up a joint from one of the cute waiters. I tried to make eye contact with one who looked like he might have some weed on him. He was dressed in the required black button-down shirt and black slacks, but something about him was laissez faire. Maybe it was his hair, longer than the other waiters, or the slight scruff under his lower lip, or the tattoo that snaked around his wrist that gave him such a bad-boy air.

I caught his eye as he headed to the kitchen with a tray full of empty glasses. He did a double take and then slowly looked me up and down before smiling.

It made me feel like a pervert.

Was he even eighteen?

I knew I didn't look my age in my black dress and stilettos, but even if I knocked off a few years, I could be his mother.

I silently sent him a message: I'm not trying to fuck you, I just want your drugs.

At that point, I became obsessed with getting high to make it through the evening, so I wasn't really very focused when the senator leaned in and repeated a question I apparently hadn't heard.

I backed up. His breath was atrocious.

Over his shoulder, I saw another VIP making a beeline for me.

Everyone wanted to talk to me tonight.

The senator was the fourth dignitary to waylay me.

For the millionth time, I tried to catch Dante's eye, but he was deep in conversation with the head of the Chamber of Commerce. Shit. It was all Dante's fault I was here. He owed me big time.

My scalp tingled a little bit, and I turned to see Nicoletta Marchese looking at me. She tossed her strawberry blonde hair and gave me a smile before turning away, leaning down toward James's wheelchair to whisper something in his ear.

My face burned.

Obviously, she'd wanted me to see.

I swallowed back the lump of jealousy. That ship had sailed years ago. He was no longer mine and never would be again. Despite what had happened.

But he was too good for her.

There was something about the willowy opera singer that made me wary.

It wasn't her fake-as-fuckness. It was something else. Something darker and more sinister.

Oliver Kingsley Hollingsworth, one of the richest men in San Francisco—and frankly one of the oldest—sidled up to her with his boy toy. Both men were gay, but that didn't stop the old geezer from caressing Nicoletta's shiny taffeta-clad ass as he went in for hugs and cheek kisses. Who knew the old boy was AC/DC?

Then the boy toy, Charles Wellington, whispered something in Nicoletta's ear. She laughed and then leaned over and kissed Old Oliver smack dab on the mouth. He gave a gruff laugh but reached out and groped her waist, pressing her up against him. What the fuck?

Were they propositioning her? Come to think of it, Dante had mentioned Hollingsworth was into some kinky shit. Dude was rich enough to pay for any depraved sex act he wanted. There were some crazy stories about the things he liked to stick his dick into. Whatever. To each their own. I just wondered if James knew what his girlfriend was up to.

I shook my head. Poor James. His wheelchair had been turned away during the whole encounter. He didn't have a clue. If that dumb bitch broke his heart, I'd kill her.

But right now, he wasn't my problem. And she wasn't worth my time or energy.

After tonight, I hoped to never see her again.

In fact, I hoped to never see 99 percent of the people in the room again. But that was just a pipe dream.

As a waiter passed, I scooped another glass of champagne off his tray and downed it.

"Miss Santangelo?"

Beatrice Stanford, a retired opera singer who liked to regale everyone with stories of her glory days, was at my side.

"It's Santella."

"Isabella?"

I gave up.

"Just call me Gia."

She cleared her throat and started over.

"Miss Gia, where is your partner, Dante?" She was looking over my shoulder. "I thought we had agreed that the salmon canapes wouldn't contain capers. They keep rolling off onto the floor."

She'd been on the board for the gala, but as far as I knew hadn't done a damn thing except give her opinion about everything and anything.

I shifted to look past her. Sure enough, there were little green balls on the carpet. Oops.

"Not sure," I said. "But I don't think Dante was in charge of the food, was he?"

I plastered a smile on my face.

As I looked over her shoulder, I made eye contact with the mayor. He was heading my way, trying to make his way through the crowd.

Shit.

The mayor had a hot nut for me since we met. We'd been on one date. It was fine. Not even a kiss goodnight. It was for the best.

In the old days, I would've fucked him in a heartbeat. But now, he made me want to run far and fast away. He was good looking, intelligent, powerful, compassionate, and funny.

In other words, dangerous as fuck.

"Excuse me!" I said to Beatrice Stanford and fled toward the kitchen.

I rushed through the swinging double doors and let out a huge over-the-top sigh.

The staff, a cook, and a few waiters looked started.

"Sorry," I said, looking for the dark-haired waiter.

He was in the back, slouched against the wall near two other waiters. They were smoking vapes. I knew what was inside the cartridges. My instincts had been right.

I pointed my finger at him and crooked it.

He pushed himself off the wall, and his friends shoved him and made snide comments.

When he got in front of me, he gave me a cocky grin.

To my surprise, he was taller than me. And even better looking close up. He exuded an animalistic sensuality. His eyes bored through me.

"At your service, Ms. Santella."

I was a little surprised he knew who I was, but didn't say anything.

Instead, I met his eyes. He licked his lips. I stared at his lips. Fuck. He was a baby. How could I look at him that way? I quickly looked away.

"I need your vape."

He grinned. "Oh yeah?"

"Yeah."

"Well, I only brought enough to get me and my boys through this night. It's all gone."

Oh, he was a cocky one, wasn't he?

"I'll make it worth your while," I said, my eyes narrowing.

"How you gonna do that?" he said, and his eyes roamed my body. "I don't need your money."

"You like your job here?" I cocked my head.

He frowned.

Shit. I'd pissed him off.

"Listen. I'm just asking for a favor here. If you could hook me up with something to get me through this god-awful night, I'd appreciate it. I'd owe you. I'd owe you a favor. I don't give favors lightly."

"Is it that bad out there?" he said, jutting his chin toward the ball room.

I sighed. "What do you think? I've got a bunch of rich fucks who think because they paid a small fortune to be here they get to tell me about their fucking bunions and stomach ulcers. Normally I would tell

them to fuck off, but since I'm on the board...and it's for a good cause."
I paused. "I have to at least be polite. It's killing me."

He nodded.

"I need to go get my stash. It's in the car. Meet me on the roof in fifteen minutes."

The last time I'd arranged to meet someone on the roof, I'd arrived to find him dead.

"Fine," I said reluctantly.

I watched him go and, despite myself, admired his long, lean body and his muscled forearms. At the last minute, he turned and caught me checking him out. My cheeks grew hot. I felt like a fucking pervert. Ugh.

As soon as I stepped out of the kitchen, I saw Dante across the room.

He was talking to James.

That's when I had to admit to myself the real reason I wanted to be drunk and high. I didn't want to face James.

Not after what had happened.

On the plane back to San Francisco from Indonesia two weeks ago, I had thought about all the people I loved who I might see again. When I thought of James, I felt a warm, nostalgic bond. I had thought my feelings for him were gone. After all, we had broken up so very long ago. He had a new life with a wife and kids.

I would always love him, but it would no longer hurt to see him.

Oh, how wrong I had been.

I had been away a long time. And a lot had changed.

He was now a widower. And someone's boyfriend.

Now, seeing him talking to Dante was like a knife in the heart.

Again.

I was regressing. Both men stopped talking and looked over at me. My heart stuttered. Then they said something and laughed.

I heard a voice say, "Gia Santella! There you are. I've been looking for you for the past hour."

Of course, he had.

It was another dude from the gala board who always stared at my tits.

But instead of wanting to run away, I now felt relief.

I turned and gave him a brilliant smile, turning toward him and placing him in front of me so he blocked my view of Dante and James.

The last thing I saw before his big head took over everything was Nicoletta in her white dress with the ugly-ass mermaid tail hem sidling up to James and putting a protective hand on the back of his wheelchair. She was staring at me with a smug fucking look the entire time.

Time to bail.

"Excuse me," I said. "I have to use the ladies room." I headed for the exit.

"Wait," I heard him say behind me. "The restrooms are the other way."

But then I slipped outside and opened the door to the stairs with my employee key card.

At the top of the stairs, the door to the roof was propped open. As I neared it, the first thing I saw was a midnight blue sky full of twinkling stars—a rare sight in San Francisco, which often had a glowing, orange night sky.

I stepped out and inhaled deeply. The air smelled like a combination of salt from the ocean breeze and the fresh greenness of forest, maybe blown over from Marin County.

Suddenly the waiter was in front of me.

Thank God. I was done with finding dead bodies for a lifetime.

He grabbed me and kissed me, pressing me back against the wall. I planted my palms on his chest and pushed him away. Hard. He was lucky I didn't demolish his balls with my knee.

"What the fuck?" I said.

"I saw the way you looked at me."

"You're just a kid," I said, not denying his words.

"I'm twenty-three."

"Like I said, 'a kid.'" But he was older than I'd thought. He actually couldn't be my son. Thank god. I'd been feeling like a pervert for the way I looked at him earlier.

"You're so sexy," he said, his hands on my waist, drawing me closer. "Let me show you how sexy I think you are."

"Where's your vape? I asked. But inwardly I groaned. His lower body pressed against mine, and I could feel his hardness and it made any resolve I had melt away.

I hadn't had sex for a long time. Since Ryder in Barcelona. That seemed like a lifetime ago. And before that, when Nico was still alive but in the care home, I went without sex for years. It was ridiculous. Sex was healthy.

I loved sex. I wanted sex. Once upon a time, I didn't even think twice about having sex with a stranger. In fact, I took pride in it.

We took turns smoking his vape. It was some damn good weed. Top notch stuff.

He handed me a joint. "You can have this for later. To remember me."

Aw, he was cute.

He leaned back toward me, his face before mine, his eyes trained on my mouth. Then his lips were on my neck.

"I think this is a bad idea," I said. Even I recognized it as the feeble protest it was.

"I don't believe you," he said in a low, husky voice. "I don't believe for one second you buy into that sexist double standard. Men can be with younger women, but women can't be with a younger guy? That's total crap."

He had a point.

His mouth was working its way up my neck. One of his hands was still firm on my waist. His other hand wrapped around the back of my neck, tangled in my hair. His breath was heavy now and I matched it. The anticipation of another kiss was irresistible. All logic and reason fled my mind. My body took over.

I could feel the heat coming off of him in waves. He leaned forward, his mouth was on mine, and despite myself I groaned in pleasure. And it just got better from there.

After, I pulled the hem of my dress back down as he buttoned up his pants.

"Holy shit," he said, still breathless.

I exhaled loudly. "Okay, maybe it actually was a really good idea."

He pulled me close and kissed me again. I let him.

Then he drew back.

"I gotta go," he said, looking over his shoulder, but still holding onto my waist. "Do you think maybe one day..."

He trailed off. He already knew the answer.

I shook my head.

Then he was gone, back down the stairs.

I walked over to the edge of the roof and looked down at the city below me.

I'd lived around the world, but this city would always be my compass point, my ground zero, my homing beacon.

Even though I'd grown up in Monterey, I hadn't felt like myself until I moved to San Francisco after my parent's murder.

It would always be home.

I rummaged around in my bag and found my pack of cigarettes and gunmetal Zippo lighter.

I pulled the joint the waiter had given me from the pack, lit it, and inhaled deeply, savoring the flavor and instant feeling of mellow gold that suffused my entire body.

At first, I was more annoyed than anything when I heard voices and the door open up behind me.

I didn't turn around. I hoped if I ignored whomever it was, they'd go away.

Then I heard the squawk of a police radio. I couldn't make out what it said.

I froze.

"Gia Santella?" a deep voice said.

Cold fear trickled through me. "Yes?"

"You're under arrest."

At first, it didn't register. Then I thought about the boy I'd been with only moments before. He'd told me he was twenty-three. And pot was legal now in California...

It took a second for me to register the rest of what the police officer had said.

"You're under arrest for murder."

1

Two weeks before

I'D FLOWN INTO—AND landed in—cities around the world, but something about landing in San Francisco was the most thrilling of all.

Every once in a while, when it was windy, the pilots would divert the plane and make this crazy landing pattern that brought the plane next to the Golden Gate bridge and then right over the Bay Bridge. It was insane.

I'm not gonna lie; it was also exhilarating.

And the thing that made it even more so, was the surge of excitement that coursed through me at coming home.

It had been years—too many years—since I'd been in San Francisco.

The sad thing was, I didn't even realize how much I missed it until the moment I saw the skyline before me and my heart clenched.

The City by the Bay was my home.

Even though I'd grown up on the sheltered, white-privileged Monterey Peninsula, I never fit in there. Despite the town really being founded by Italians, the rich white kids I went to school with looked down on me.

They all assumed my father was in the mafia.

I really should thank them for my martial arts skills, though.

After they spat racial slurs at me, I got in a fight at school. After that, my dad had me take private martial arts lessons. But I still was never comfortable at school. I was always an outsider.

It didn't help that I was olive skinned and dark-haired, while my asshole brother was blonde. My classmates loved him and hated me. It made sense since he hated me. He was a sociopathic monster. When he was murdered, I never shed a tear. May he rot in hell.

As the plane bumped to a landing, I sent a text to my driver, Tony.

Tony was a grandfather now. He had prison tattoos and had done time for murder. I could trust him with my life.

I grabbed my gunmetal gray carryon bag and got off the plane, heading straight through the airport, eager to see my old driver and friend.

I walked as fast as I could in those damned high-heeled black suede boots. For some reason, I'd thought it would be a good idea to dress up for the trip home. Maybe because years ago when I left the city, I'd been dressed in worn leather pants and a ripped T-shirt with a skull and crossbones that said, "Fuck Authority."

That Gia was gone.

I was a grown damn woman now.

I laughed at my own thoughts. Who was I fooling? I still felt nineteen.

But my style had improved.

I still loved leather pants, and actually was wearing some, but they were sleek as butter and cost a small fortune. Unless you looked closely, you might not even know they were leather.

My huge, dark sunglasses, which had been on the entire flight, shielded my face from the few people I caught staring at me. It was a little odd. Did I stand out that much? For most of my life, I'd tried to blend in.

When people stared at me, it was because I wanted them to and had worn a short skirt or low-cut top for just that reason.

Now, dressed in expertly tailored leather pants, a fitted black blouse, and my boots, I didn't see what the big deal was.

As soon as I stepped outside, I took a deep breath of the salty air I'd always loved.

San Francisco.

Tony was there in front of me. He'd hopped out of the massive black SUV and was reaching for my carryon.

I squealed like a little girl and wrapped him in a hug. And then I drew back grinning like a fool.

"Man, it's been a long-ass time since I saw your mug," I said.

He gave me a shy grin and looked down. "Same."

"Thank you for coming to get me. I know you're big time now, and I appreciate you taking the time," I said.

"Gia. You're my girl. I drop everything for you."

For some reason, his words brought a tear to my eye.

"Thanks, man," I said in a gruff voice.

Then I was in the passenger seat, fiddling with the radio. He hopped in.

"You're listening to Al Green?" I said in a pseudo-shocked voice. "Have you gone soft?"

He laughed. I connected my iPhone.

"I'm gonna blow your mind," I said and pressed play on some Cardi B.

I rolled down the window and cranked up the volume and leaned back, closing my eyes during the drive into the city. Once, I peeked over at Tony and saw him tapping his fingernails on the steering wheel. When I realized I wasn't torturing him with my music, I closed my eyes again.

After a while, the sounds of the city made me open my eyes. We were downtown now, in the deep shadows created by the skyscrapers around us. My loft and building in the Tenderloin was just north of us, but I'd asked Tony to take me to a hotel near Union Square.

My friend Danny had been living in my loft and managing my building and its tenants for the past several years. I couldn't wait to see him and the Tenderloin area again, but I wanted to chill out and explore the city on my own for a few hours first.

Besides, what was I going to do, kick Danny out of his home now that I was back? No way. I would find a new place to rent in the T.L. The loft was his. I'd make it official as soon as I saw him. He had no idea I was coming home, anyway. I hadn't wanted him to worry about me trying to move back in.

My pal Danny was a world-class hacker and drone expert. He'd become emancipated at seventeen—with my help—because of a fucked-up home life. He'd saved my butt more times than I could count.

When I left San Francisco, I offered him my loft in exchange for managing the entire building. Meeting with him was on my list of things to do now that I was back in town

We were almost to the hotel. I realized I was starving. And wanted nothing more than some San Francisco clam chowder in a bread bowl. It was my comfort food.

"Hey, you hungry?" I said, turning down the music.

He shrugged. "I'm a dude. I can always eat."

"Do you have time to swing by the wharf? I'm buying."

"I took the rest of the day off. I didn't know where we were going or what you needed."

I made a note to pay him for the entire day. But meanwhile, my mouth was watering.

"Let's go then. I'm ravenous. I haven't had a bowl of chowder for years."

2

Mayor Anthony Ferraro hated that he had to be surrounded by bodyguards.

He was trying to walk through the airport like a goddamn normal person and yet they flanked him as though some maniac was going to scream like a banshee and charge him with a butcher knife. For chrissakes, they'd already gone through security. The only people with weapons were law enforcement or TSA.

But he knew his irritation was misplaced. And that it was the smart thing to do.

After that threat on his life last week, everyone in his campaign was rattled.

It had been a pretty specific threat too.

At least one other member of the opera gala fundraising committee had received the same threat. But unlike that threat, this one had proved that the person knew where he lived.

Like the threat that his colleague on the gala fundraising committee had received, he was told that unless he shut down the opera, he would pay with his life.

It was ridiculous.

He'd been brought up to speed about the earlier controversy surrounding the opera in New York City as soon as he was asked to be on the committee last year, but recently, the threats had come to his city as the date of the performance grew closer.

The San Francisco Opera was now in rehearsals for *The Death of Engleberg*, which had sparked protests during its New York opening by those claiming the performance was anti-Semitic and glorified terrorism.

The opera was about the 1985 hijacking of an Italian cruise ship by terrorists. During the hijacking, a Jewish man, Leon Engleberg, who used a wheelchair, was murdered by the terrorists. After the New York premiere, Engleberg's two daughters released a statement condemning the opera saying, "We are outraged at the exploitation of our parents and the coldblooded murder of our father as the centerpiece of a production that appears to us to be anti-Semitic."

As soon as the San Francisco opera announced that its season would feature the opera, protests began. Now that the opera had started rehearsals, thinly veiled threats had been sent to the singers, members of the opera's board of directors, the opera gala fundraising committee, and various members of the San Francisco Opera Association. The FBI and San Francisco Police Department had actually assigned security details to the opera and its members.

While the mayor would not give in to the demands to cancel or condemn the opera, he did agree to the precautions his campaign staff insisted upon.

He was no stranger to hostile people. Growing up as a politician's son had exposed him to all sorts of unhinged whack jobs. The difference was this person knew where he lived.

"Sir?" One of his bodyguards was herding him. He'd been so lost in thought, he'd not followed their strict orders to stick to the side of the concourse.

He looked up to do a course correction and froze. He stopped dead in his tracks.

The woman coming toward him wasn't the most beautiful woman he'd ever seen—or been with for that matter—but she seemed the most...he tried to put his finger on the word...most sensual? Maybe that was it. But it was more.

She was sensual and exuded something that he could only describe as unbridled power.

And he loved power. Power was his drug. It was what he lived for.

He could identify it in another person instantly.

And this woman had it.

It was intoxicating.

He watched her pass and then turned his head, mesmerized.

"Sir?"

"What?" he said, unintentionally snapping at the man at his shoulder. "Sorry. I...I..." he trailed off. What was he going to say? He was in love? He was struck dumb at seeing a beautiful woman?

Finally, he formed some words.

"Who was that?"

"Who, sir?" the man said, glancing behind them. He looked too. She was gone.

"Never mind."

As he strode through the airport, heads turned.

He was used to it.

As the youngest mayor of one of the country's biggest cities, he had been on the cover of magazines and on the front page of newspapers around the world.

His face was a little too recognizable, he thought.

But it was all part of the job.

His father had been a rock star. Politicians across the country still talked about him.

He needed to carve out his own identity.

While his father would consider it beneath him to stop and talk to plebeians on the street, Mayor Ferraro made a point to do that.

That's why, when a woman came up to him at the airport, he lifted a hand for his bodyguards to let her approach.

"Mayor Ferraro," the woman said. "I just want you to know that you have changed my life."

He smiled and tilted his head, waiting.

She blurted the rest of the story out.

Apparently, she'd been down in the dumps and homeless, and when he had approved the permanent homeless camp on Van Ness Street and ordered job training workshops held there every Friday, she had taken the workshop and turned her life around.

Now, she was working full time as an office manager and had her own apartment.

"I owe all of it to you," she said. "I don't know how I can ever thank you."

Then she licked her lips and looked at him, and he knew exactly how she wanted to thank him.

Fuck.

At first, having willing women throw themselves at him had been exciting. But now he craved more of a challenge. Not that the woman wasn't delectable. She would probably be sensational in bed, but he was over sensational. He wanted someone who would challenge him intellectually as well. He sighed. That was tougher to find.

For the past year, he'd found just that with Merilee Conley.

A beautiful black woman with as much power, if not more, than he had. And to make it even more enticing, she was kind and just and fun to be around.

But best of all, she was his equal. A powerful state Attorney

General whose brain turned him on as much as the playboy body she hid under tailored suits. But her career was more important than their relationship, and they'd broken it off when she relocated to Sacramento.

As he thought about her, he realized this woman in front of him was still talking. He focused back on the conversation. "Thank you for letting me know. But I fear you give me more credit that I deserve," he said, smoothly. "It's stories like this that motivate me to keep up the fight. I'm sorry but I have a pressing engagement, so I really must go."

On cue by his words, the bodyguards took over, moving her away and clearing a path for him to continue his getting-longer-by-the-minute walk to the car. He heard the woman saying in a last-ditch effort. "I work for the county if you ever want to talk more or need a volunteer on your campaign."

He tried to ignore it. She was tempting, but she'd end up hurt. He could never see her as more than a brief night of pleasure. He was tired of letting women down gently. He was always honest with them—telling them up front in his very diplomatic way that essentially he was only there for the one-time sex, but still they held out hopes that they would be the one to change him."

He sighed. If only, he could meet someone who was his equal. A woman who didn't need a man. A woman who simply wanted a man and took one when she wanted.

Despite himself, he couldn't stop thinking about the woman who had walked by. He bet she didn't need a man.

"Sir, we're running late."

"Clear the way."

On his words, the bodyguards spoke into their cell phones, and within seconds, TSA agents and police officers had cleared a path for him to sweep through the crowded airport.

If that wasn't power, he didn't know what was. He tried not to let it go to his head as he walked straight past the luggage carousels and stepped out onto the sidewalk, where his driver opened his car door.

Another bodyguard would gather the luggage and follow in another car.

He leaned his head on the headrest and closed his eyes.

He had to find out who that woman was.

He wanted her.

And whatever he wanted, he got.

3

CHARLES WELLINGTON WINKED AS HE JOGGED BY THE OLDER woman walking her dog. She giggled like a schoolgirl. He had that effect on people.

Men, women, boys, girls, small dogs. They all loved him.

Even now, in Lululemon jogging shorts with sweat pouring down his face.

Only four more blocks until he reached his Pacific Heights home and then he could take a long, hot shower.

Sweating disgusted him. But having the body he did was worth the disgusting smell and slickness that came with keeping in top form.

So, each day he ran, morning and night. And each day he worked out, lifting the barbell until his muscles strained and popped. He'd stare at himself in the mirror sometimes, admiring his muscle tone. No wonder everyone wanted to fuck him.

He had never been the smartest guy around, but he knew how to make the most of what he was given. And from a young age, he knew his biggest asset was his body and good looks. He had thick dirty blonde hair and big puppy-brown eyes that made him look innocent, especially when he was between someone's legs and looked up, fluttering his long black eyelashes. Instant orgasm.

His father had taught him to make the most of what God had given him. He'd said, "Son, we need to do the best with what we've been given."

But his father, dumb old fool, had also encouraged him to settle for a small, simple life.

Maybe that had been okay for his parents, but as soon as he got a taste of the good life, he never looked back.

His poor father must be rolling over in the grave since he died knowing that part of the good life that Charles lived involved putting another man's cock in his mouth. Too bad. Didn't dear old Dad realize he'd made him that way? When Charles had been caught having gay sex to pay for his prom date, his father had kicked him out of the house.

At that point in his life, having sex for money was the only thing that kept Charles alive.

It wasn't his favorite thing, but selling his body had paid the bills. It was how he lived in this mansion with the indoor pool and elevator. It was how he would become filthy rich.

It never meant that he had lost the desire to taste the sweetness of a woman.

And he must have matured, because there was only one woman he wanted. He wanted her so bad he would crawl inside her skin and be her if he had the chance.

She was intoxicating.

And glory of glories, she loved him back. With a furious passion he hadn't known existed. And it was all for him.

If he did as she wanted.

And if he could bide his time.

Because she had dreams as big as his.

And making them come true would not be easy. But together they could do it.

When they were together, they could do anything.

He unlocked the door to his apartment and ran up the last few flights of stairs. No reason to wimp out now this close to the finish line.

That applied to their plans, as well.

Even though the end was in sight, he wasn't sure he could put up with it much longer.

At times, if he allowed himself to think about it, the whole thing made him sick.

What got him going each day was thoughts of a future with his true love. He'd promised her so much. Their dream life was just around the corner. They would live like a king and queen. Fuck all night and sleep all day. He would rub her feet with that special lotion made from crushed diamonds and bathe her body in the most expensive perfumes. He would wash her hair every day himself.

But a lot of people had to die before he could make good on his word.

Mostly, one man had to die.

The one man who stood in his way. The one man who stood between him and a future that most people could only dream about.

Each day, the only thing that kept him going was to imagine, vividly, the man's murder. He couldn't wait to see the man bleed to death, alone, looking up at him with hatred.

All in good time.

Then he could be with his true love.

There were so many obstacles in their way, but true love would conquer all.

One by one, they would die at his hands. And someone else would pay for it while he rode off into the sunset with his love. And no one would be the wiser.

It was funny; he had never realized that he had the stomach for murder. Who knew?

He was less worried about the actual killing and more worried about getting caught.

But he had a foolproof plan to get away with it.

One that was so crazy insane nobody would believe it in a million years.

Thank god he'd kept in touch with his Army buddy. And luckily his Army buddy was one of the smartest dudes alive. And luckily, he still liked getting his dick sucked.

His beautiful lover wasn't crazy about the idea, but she knew they were both going through the motions and doing what was necessary to create the future of their dreams.

4

When I got to the hotel, I was fat and happy.

It had been great to catch up with Tony and hear about him becoming a grandfather. He'd lost touch with his kids when they were young because he'd been in prison. It was heartwarming to hear that he'd been forgiven and given a second chance as a very involved grandfather.

He watched the grandkids during the day and drove at night. Usually.

He'd made an exception for me. I scolded him.

"Family first. Always."

"It's cool," he said. "I can still drive you during the day now that I'm back. Grandma likes to have the kids to herself for a few hours. They can do girlie things—get their nails done, all that bullshit stuff I hate."

I sighed and took another big bite of clam chowder. "Fine. But family first."

"I get it. I get it," he said.

Now, on the curb of the hotel, he handed the valet my suitcase, and I stood on tiptoe to give him a kiss on his grizzly cheek.

"Thanks for everything, old friend," I said.

He mumbled something gruff and got back in the car. He got embarrassed by sentimental stuff.

I was already checked in on the mobile app, so when I stepped into the elevator, I hit the hotel suite button and let the laser scan my code. Dante had also arranged for me to have an "employee key card" on my phone to access other parts of the hotel if necessary.

It made sense. In less than a month, if all went as planned, we would be the new owners of the hotel.

The elevator opened directly into a private hallway. There were two doors. One to the rooftop Jacuzzi and one to my suite.

My suitcase was already sitting in front of the door to the suite.

I opened up the door and was greeted by golden hour sunlight. It was such a welcome change from the gloomy, shadowy streets below. Once upon a time, San Francisco's gray skies and shadows had comforted me. Now, after living in Mexico, San Diego, and Barcelona, I craved sunshine.

Being in the hotel suite was almost like taking off from a cloudy day in an airplane and then rising above the clouds into the glorious, heavenly sunshine.

I could get used to it.

And Dante knew that.

Somehow, he'd convinced me to go in with him in buying the hotel. I was pretty sure we could get financing from the company I owned. But we had another obstacle in our way. The current owner agreed to sell to us, but had one strange condition first—exposing an employee who had betrayed him.

While I'm sure Dante loved the idea of owning a boutique hotel, the truth is, what he was most interested in was the Michelin three-star restaurant that was the true penthouse of the hotel.

It had spectacular views and world-class dining.

Dante already owned several successful restaurants, but to him, this was the crème de la crème.

"Come on, Gia," he'd said a few days before. "You are going to be bored out of your pretty skull unless you have a project to tackle."

"What's so challenging about plunking down a wad of cash and buying a hotel. Boring. Snore."

"There's some underhanded shit going on there," he said in a low voice.

I was instantly intrigued. Dante never swore. If he used the word "shit" that meant whatever was going on was a royal clusterfuck of massive proportions.

"Do tell?"

"Someone is embezzling from the current owner. His name is Gunther. Herr Gunther Janson. He lives in Berlin. For whatever reason, he likes me."

"Is he gay?"

"What?" Dante said, annoyed. "What does that have to do with it? You don't have to be gay to like me, Gia."

"I was just wondering."

He ignored me.

"So, you'd have to live undercover there for a while to figure out who is behind it all."

I was starting to like the idea more and more.

"Undercover?"

"Gunther has a house in Napa too. One of his many houses. He likes to come visit his vineyard once a year. He's been coming to my restaurant for years. He asked me over to his place and gave me the pitch. He wants to sell, but he wants to unearth the employee who betrayed him first. He said if I can figure out who it is, he will sell to us at a bargain price."

"Huh," I said. "So, if you can figure out whose fucking him, he'll give us a deal?"

"Exactly," Dante said, his voice excited. "But I can't do it on my own."

So, now I was checking into the hotel suite as a guest, when really, I was a fucking spy! I loved it. I was excited to be all James Bond and shit. What that entailed, I wasn't really sure yet. But it would come to me.

The Hotel suite was mostly a wide-open, sunny space. Double doors led to a master bedroom and bath.

I wheeled my suitcase into the bedroom. The bed was hanging from massive steel cables attached to the edges of a skylight that took up most of the ceiling. I could just imagine the starlight that would shine down at night. I was already excited for bed.

Everything in the hotel suite was sleek, yet warm. For instance, while the couches had clean, modern lines, the material was plush gray velvet.

The bed had light gray silk sheets and a darker gray velvet duvet cover.

Thick white fur throws were tossed on both the couches and the bed.

The dining room table was black marble with white leather chairs pulled up to it.

I walked around, touching all the materials. It was as if the hotel suite had been designed with me in mind. I loved the sensuality of how things felt.

No scratchy wool sweaters for me. Soft-as-butter leather pants, silky blouses, velvet blazers? Yes, please.

I stepped out onto the balcony that ran the length of the hotel suite facing the Golden Gate bridge. Spectacular view. But cold.

I came back inside and stripped on my way to the bedroom, throwing my clothes on the floor behind me as I walked.

After a long, hot shower to wash the travel filth off me, I

dressed in comfy yoga pants and a tee, poured myself a Bourbon from the mirrored bar, and settled onto the chaise lounge facing the TV. I flicked through the channels and settled on an entertainment show based in Hollywood. I needed light, mindless escapism.

Hearing about the exploits of movie stars was always fun.

This episode was just beginning as I settled in. The host, a gorgeous woman—unfortunately dressed in an ugly, frilly pink chiffon number that only an aged hooker would wear—promised the latest on the duchess (apparently a former maid accused her of racism, which I doubted was true), how Deepfake technology had made it appear that Tom Cruise was eating lollipops on TikTok (it was mind-blowing and terrifying how that video technology could make someone dangerous like Vladimir Putin appear to say things he never said), and how a hot affair had destroyed a storybook marriage between two Oscar-winning movie stars.

I was all in.

Getting caught up in the dramas of celebrities was a fitting escape. My own life had been filled with so much dark, deep shit, that the fluffy crap they had to deal with was comical. I mean, sure, it was still serious, but cry me a river. Boo-hoo, someone is impersonating you on TikTok, Tom. And sorry, Meghan, that you're accused of shit you didn't do while you are living in LA hobnobbing with celebs. And what a rough break, that your celebrity marriage ended.

By the time the show was over, I'd made and finished another drink and was feeling no pain. I was also exhausted. I'd fought my jet lag as long as I could so I could try to get back on a normal schedule. The long travel day from Indonesia had finally caught up with me. There hadn't been any direct flights, so I'm pretty sure I'd lost a day or two in getting back. It was all a big blur. I'd slept on both flights, so I was really disoriented when the pilot finally announced we were on our descent into San Francisco.

All I knew was that if I stayed awake a few more hours I'd have half a shot at getting back on a normal West Coast sleep schedule.

I decided to crawl into bed before I ended up sleeping on the couch.

I woke with a start at three in the morning. Damn. I knew it was late in Sumatra. Might as well not fight it. I guess I was lucky to get the sleep I did. At least if I got up now, there was a good chance I'd be tired at the normal time tonight.

For a second, I wondered what time it was in Southern France.

Where Ryder was.

I'd jumped in bed with him sort of on the rebound after Nico's death. But what I'd found in him scared me. He got me. Like Nico, he knew I'd killed people. And, also like Nico, so had he. But he got me on some scary-as-fuck profound level. Like he could see right through my soul.

I hated it. And I loved it.

But I ran away from it.

He has his own life in France.

I'd thought I'd never see him again.

But then before leaving Sumatra, I'd called him and asked if he'd ever been to San Francisco. Now he was trying to figure out a way to come out here to visit me.... I couldn't even think about that yet. I had too much to do here first.

Today would be busy. I had plans to meet with Dante for the board meeting of our company and then later, we'd go to dinner. Somewhere in the next week, I wanted to swing by the Tenderloin neighborhood and talk to Danny.

As soon as I finished my undercover work here at the hotel, I'd have to go house hunting in the Tenderloin. I wasn't sure what I wanted yet—an apartment or an actual house. It depended on what was available, I guess.

Even though it was still dark, I was wide awake in bed, my mind racing with all these thoughts of what I needed to do that day.

That's when I looked up.

Holy shit. The stars were amazing. I couldn't believe I was in the middle of a big city and this was my night sky. I sat there in awe for a few minutes, feeling inconsequential faced with the sheer awesomeness of the universe above me.

I'd lost so much in my life. So many people I loved had been taken violently from me.

I'd come back to San Francisco because I felt lost and adrift.

The most compelling reason for my return was an utter, all-encompassing loneliness.

My family was too busy for me. Eva had her own busy life in Italy running her female assassin boot camp. Rose didn't want me in her life right then. I knew on some level that this was her attempt to forge her own life. It hurt, but I knew enough about my own journey as a young woman that I had to let her go. I knew she would return to me.

In desperation, I'd called Dante. And he did what he always does—told me what I needed to hear. He told me to come home.

As usual, he was right. It was annoying how often this was the case.

Here I was in San Francisco. And even though I missed the hell out of the people I'd lost—my parents, my first love, Bobby, my greatest love, Nico—I knew I was going to be OK.

Now, lying in bed looking at the star-filled sky above me, I also knew that I was never truly alone. Those I had loved were out there somewhere. I knew it deep in my soul.

5

Nicoletta Marchese sat primly on the small stool in front of the vanity and examined her face. Her silky strawberry-blonde hair was pulled into a messy bun on top of her head. She'd removed her stage makeup and was spreading moisturizer onto her porcelain smooth cheeks. Her black eyes were stripped of makeup, but her lashes were still lush and dark.

She was the most beautiful woman he'd ever seen.

"Did they bother you tonight?" Charles Hollingsworth asked, his eyes squinting.

"Not really," she said. "We all left the back way. The guy you hired to drive us was there, and it went smoothly. Nobody was any the wiser."

Ever since the opera had announced it would be premiering *The Death of Engleberg,* a bevy of violent protesters had begun to appear every night in front of the theater. So far, the protesters had been fairly peaceful, mostly holding signs, but lately they had startled to heckle people.

And then last week, it had gotten violent. A protester had attacked one of the singers leaving late at night. The man had been beaten to a pulp and a note had been sent to the newspapers saying that unless the performance was canceled, someone would die.

"It's fine," she said again. "It gives us the perfect motive."

They'd been plotting the murder for six months, waiting for the perfect time and circumstance. The protester's threats had suddenly given them the cover they needed to commit the murder.

He hated leaving her vulnerable. But that was also part of their plan. He had to pretend like he was in love with someone else. That meant being at someone else's beck and call and pretending he wasn't madly in love with Nicoletta.

"I can't do this anymore," he said and paced the apartment. "We belong together. The thought of you fucking that gimp...I can't handle it."

"Fuck you," she said lightly and took another drag off the joint in her fingers. "Just because he has a bigger dick than you."

He was in front of her in a second, chest heaving, eyes wild.

"I'm just kidding," she said. "Don't be a pussy. You know you're the only man for me. Besides do I complain about you getting fucked by someone else?"

He didn't answer.

"Listen," he said. "I know our original plan was just to do the one murder, but it will be too obvious."

"What are you saying?" she said. She was clearly irritated.

"Do you want to get away with this or not?"

"Uh, yeah," she said sarcastically. "That's why I'm fucking someone else. It was your idea, remember? I'm just doing what I'm told."

"Okay, okay," Charles said. "I apologize. It's just hard for me to swallow sometimes. We need that cop in our pocket if we're going to get away with this. It's just one more thing to tip the scales in our favor."

"Don't worry," she said, examining her eyebrows in the mirror over the vanity. "He's my bitch. He believes everything I say. He'll do anything for me."

"Well, as I was saying... We need to kill at least two other random people, too, so nobody can figure out the motive. If three people die and the detectives think it's because they all have something in common, they won't look at us."

"What? Speak English," she said, closing her eyes.

"We kill three people on the gala fundraising committee," he said. "That way they think it's connected to the protests."

She raced over, jumping up and wrapping her legs around his waist. You are a genius, Charles."

He laughed and clutched her tight.

He spun her around. There was a drug deal going down on the street below. He drew back a little. He couldn't wait until he could get Nicoletta out of this shithole neighborhood. She reached for the joint he had set down in the ashtray, but he plucked it out of her hand before she could bring it to her mouth.

"Hey," she squealed. "Bring that back. I'm not done with it yet."

He set her down gently and pushed her a little bit away from him.

"You are now. Now get naked."

She groaned. "You're so bossy."

But she gave him a sexy smile. Keeping her eyes trained on his, she slowly slid the straps of her slip so they fell down her shoulders, revealing pure white flesh.

He held his breath, watching. He could feel the electricity between them.

She sure knew how to put on a show. He suddenly ached with desire. Her breasts were large, and her ass was even larger.

Her vanilla skin was creamy and soft. There was no place he'd rather be than between her silky, slick thighs.

"Jesus."

"What?" she said and shrugged. But he caught sight of a smile as she turned away. She climbed up onto his bed on all fours. She was facing away from him, and he was already unbuttoning his pants when she tossed her long red hair and looked back at him.

"Come and give me some special attention."

He didn't wait for another invite.

When he woke later in the dark, her leg and an arm was tossed over him. He reached for his phone without waking her. There was a text message. He couldn't believe it. It was the answer to his prayers. He had to get on his computer immediately. He tried to gently move her arm and legs to sit up, but her eyes fluttered open.

"Where you going?" she said in a voice husky with sleep.

"I've got to call Marshall."

She sat up "What's up?"

"Just a second," he said, distracted.

A few seconds later, she joined him at the small desk. Their faces glowed in the blue light.

"What is that?" she said. "I don't get it. It shows you fucking Marshall? I thought you said you said you guys never experimented like that in college.... Wait. That's not college. That's him *now* with his shaved head!" She whirled. He caught her arm.

"Look at the date and time," he said.

"Fuck you," she said. But she turned around. He started the video over. As Marshall got fucked from behind by her boyfriend, he suddenly turned and grinned at the camera and held up a newspaper. It was a Geneva newspaper with today's date. Marshall lived in Geneva.

Her eyes widened. "That's today's newspaper. But that's impossible."

"That's right," he said. He couldn't hide his grin. "That's how we are going to get away with murder."

6

The morning passed quickly.

I spent it preparing for the board meeting at my father's... well, now *my* company with Dante. We were pitching them on backing our purchase of the hotel.

I spent the first few hours going over reports for my father's company so I wouldn't seem like a rookie when I walked into the board meeting.

My morning was spent fueled by espresso as I skimmed documents trying to play catch up after years of ignoring and neglecting the company. I'd put good, solid people in place to run it while I was out of the country, and I didn't regret the job they had done.

I was basically a figurehead there, now, but it still helped to have my finger on the pulse when I walked in. I didn't have the heart to sell the company, since it was my father's pride and joy. His legacy lived on through the company and the foundations it supported, including the nonprofit—Ethel's Place–that I'd formed to help homeless people get on their feet again.

Now, Dante and I were going to propose that the board loan

us some of the hotel purchase money. We had some of the money, but not all of it. A lot of my capital was tied up.

Dante had prepared our presentation, so I also had to go over that again, even though I'd studied it on the flights from overseas.

By eleven, I was ready to shower and get ready for the board meeting.

Dante texted me that he was on his way down from his home in wine country and would swing by the hotel to pick me up.

I couldn't wait to see him!

He'd made several trips to Europe to visit me over the years, but now we lived in the same state. I intended to spend way more time with him and his husband, Wayne. They split time between Wayne's home in San Diego and Dante's spread up north.

After I slicked on black eyeliner and a nude lipstick, I buttoned up a white silk blouse and then pulled on my Armani trousers and matching black wool blazer. Even with a few buttons undone on the blouse, it still felt a little stiff, so along with my Louboutin red-soled pumps, I looped a few thick gold chains of different lengths around my neck.

For good luck, I slipped on the massive red ruby ring Nico had bought me for our ten-year anniversary. It brought a lump to my throat to see it on my finger but also made me feel a surge of gratefulness that I had experienced such a great love in my life.

I stuffed some papers in my dad's worn and beaten leather attaché case and headed for the lobby.

Dante pulled up in a G Wagon, which made me grin. He never changed.

Jumping out, he ran over and grabbed me in such an exuberant hug, I let out an involuntary squeal and then burst into laughter. Drawing back, I held him at arm's length.

Still a looker. He seemed to be more handsome with age.

"I love you, Dante!" I said spontaneously.

He laughed and kissed my cheek.

"You look amazing, bella."

Twenty minutes later, we flung open the doors to the boardroom and strode in like we owned the place. Well, we did, but still, it felt great to walk into the room and see so many familiar faces.

Two hours later, we had the backing we needed.

Dante held it in until we were in the elevator and then he threw up his arm in a victory salute.

"I'm going to make this hotel and restaurant the most happening, sought-after place in the San Francisco Bay Area. People are going to fly in from around the world just to have a meal there," he said with a grin, his white teeth flashing attractively against his olive skin.

"You'll do it too," I said.

"You ready to revamp the management there?" he said. "Get rid of the dead weight and bring in some movers and shakers?"

"I've been thinking about it nonstop," I said. "We will offer the most luxurious experience of any hotel out there. Anyone can furnish their hotels in expensive accoutrements, but we're going to be the only ones who offer a completely luxurious, pampering experience and the best service on the planet."

As Dante drove us home, he kept smiling. "What are you thinking?"

"Every room is a hotel suite."

"What?" Dante laughed. "That's impossible."

"Yes, but we can give every guest a taste of the hotel suite experience," I said. "The hotel has fifty floors, right? And the building has four sides, right?"

"Keep going." He leaned forward and looked up at the

skyscrapers surrounding us in the downtown area. Cars were stopped in a line in front of us. It was rush hour.

"What if instead of 1,000 rooms and two hotel suites like it has now, we make 200 rooms. That would mean four rooms per floor. Each room would have sweeping views on two full walls."

"I'm getting it," Dante said, tapping the steering wheel with his fingers.

"Depending on which room you have, you would get one of four views: The Golden Gate, The Pacific Ocean, The Bay Bridge, or Radio Tower. Obviously, the most expensive rooms would be with Golden Gate views, the least expensive the Radio Tower. People would book their rooms by views: Golden Gate, Sunset, Bay Bridge, Radio Tower."

Dante was quiet for a few seconds and then he punched the steering wheel.

"Brilliant," he said. "The hotel is already known as having the best views in the city, so now we capitalize on it to the max."

"Exactly," I said. "And then we make each room ultra-luxurious—like my hotel suite but even more over-the-top. Each room will have a small fireplace, and the beds will have eiderdown comforters and guests can choose their pillows from a menu. The furniture will be velvet and leather and covered in fur throws. There will be monogrammed bathrobes and each suite will have a Nespresso machine and a small cocktail bar. Guests can request their own personal makeup artist, hair stylist, barber, and manicurist to come to their suite. Guests can have a bubble bath, or they can request a champagne, rose petal, or even chocolate bath."

"Oh Gia, you're so naughty."

I smiled, but didn't pause.

Dante pulled up in front of the hotel.

"Question?"

I raised an eyebrow.

"What does the guest in the real hotel suite get that makes her feel special?"

"Well, just so you know, I'm not designing this to attract the old, stuffy rich people. I want the edgy, adventurous rich. Whether they are twenty or eighty. So, if you are staying in one of the top three hotel suites, you get your own Ferrari to drive during your stay; you also get your own personal butler at your beck and call—the butler will draw your bath, pack your suitcase, iron your clothes, or whatever, and a free helicopter ride that takes off from the roof's helipad and flies over the Golden Gate bridge at sunset."

"You're a fucking genius, Santella."

"I know, right?" I said.

I was reaching for the door handle when he said. "I'm glad you want to buy the hotel with me."

"Me too."

I started to open the door.

"There's just one more thing."

Oh shit. I could tell by his tone that I wasn't going to like what he was about to say.

"There's this gala, a fundraiser for the San Francisco Opera, that's being held in the restaurant next week."

He paused.

I lifted my eyebrow. "Okay? Is that a problem?"

"Because we are planning to buy the hotel, I volunteered us both to be on the fundraising committee."

"You're kidding me?"

"Nope. I've been on it for six months. You're going to join me now. There's only one more meeting anyway. It will be a good chance for you to meet some of the city's movers and shakers."

"You know I hate shit like that. I hate the board of the company *I* own. I hate everything to do with it. It's usually a bunch of people putting on airs and acting like their shit don't stink and arguing over which fucking caviar to serve!" I said in a single stream of words.

Dante nodded seriously. "I know. But I need you there. Besides, it's another way for us to get to know more people at the hotel and figure out who is embezzling. I need your street smarts."

"My street smarts?" I said in a mocking voice.

"Whatever. You know what I mean," he said, exasperated. "Please, Gia. We need to figure out who's stealing from the hotel. All the big players in the hotel's management are on the committee, along with some politicians and opera people. It's a great opportunity to get to know the players in the city, as well. We're going to need them on our side to do the remodeling. I need your help."

"Fine. Only for you."

"There's more."

Oh shit again. "What?" The fundraising committee's meeting is tonight," he looked down at his TAG Heuer watch.

"In four hours, actually. I'll be at your door ten minutes early."

I glared at him.

"One other thing," he said.

"You're fucking kidding, right?"

"One of the committee members turned up dead this morning. They're investigating his death as suspicious. It's pretty suspect given the animosity toward the opera house right now."

"Hold up. No clue what you're talking about. Remember, I've been overseas."

Dante filled me in, telling me about the controversial musical, *The Death of Engleberg*, the New York protests, and the death threats.

Dante kept speaking, but all I could think was: San Francisco Police Department. Wheelchair. Death threats.

James.

One of the great loves in my life. And now I was in the same city as him.

He'd received death threats trying to expose corrupt cops in the San Francisco police department. Then, one of his own brothers in blue had shot and paralyzed him, condemning him to a wheelchair for the rest of his life.

We were ill-fated lovers: He was a man of the law. I was a killer.

We'd tried to make it work and ended up friends. But he would always own a small piece of my heart. I needed to call him and tell him I was in town. Maybe I'd invite him and his wife, Genevieve out to dinner. I wondered how old their baby was now and if they had had other children. It would be good to see them. It would no longer sting to see James happy as a family man—which was all he ever wanted. It was all I ever wanted *for* him. But it was something I couldn't give him.

I tuned back in. "Where was dude's security detail when he was whacked?"

"Dude? His name is Sam Glass. Or was. The security detail is based at the opera house—mainly to make sure performers leave rehearsals and get safely to their cars. Up until now, the worst of it had been protesters trying to block the entrances and exits of the opera house and a few rotten eggs thrown."

"Classy."

"Right?" Dante said and tapped the steering wheel again with his manicured fingernails. It was his nervous habit. "But obviously, it might have escalated if Glass was murdered."

"Good times," I said. "And for some reason you thought I should serve on the committee for the opera's fundraising gala, so now suddenly this is my concern?"

Dante sighed loudly, clearly exasperated.

This wasn't my crisis.

"Gia. Serving on the committee for the gala is going to be the very best way to get to know the movers and shakers in San Francisco. If you're going to own a hotel, you are going to want to be friends with them."

"Be friends? Do you even know me?"

"At least pretend to like them," he said. "It will go a long way in getting everything approved for our remodel. Plus, the gala is in two weeks. We've been working on this for a year. In other words, all the hard work is done. All you have to do is show up and act nice. Which I know is going to be tough for you."

"Fine," I bit the word out, half joking, half serious. "For you, Dante. I'll do it for you."

"Thank you."

7

Back in my room, I ordered a bottle of Pellegrino and a charcuterie board and started doing some deep dives into the backgrounds the hotel management team. If someone was crooked, it would probably be one of them. They were the only ones with the power and access to embezzle the hundred grand that had gone missing.

After looking at start dates and backgrounds, I narrowed it down to three people who could possibly be embezzling. They had means and motive. And sure enough, all three were on the gala board. Dante was right. It was a good spot for me to be.

I examined the three names:

Maxwell Carlton, the general manager of the hotel.

Stuart McBride, the food and beverage director.

Cynthia Turner, the hotel maintenance engineer.

I'd have Danny find out more—pull all their financial information. That way we'd know if one of them was suddenly flush enough to buy a new home or if any of them was deep in debt.

I shot him a quick text. I didn't tell him I was in town. He was used to getting my requests for help from around the world. I'd surprise him in person.

After getting a cramped neck sitting on my bed hunched over my laptop, I decided all suites in the new hotel would have small tucked-away desks with business centers built in.

I decided to go for a nice long walk to wake up.

On my walk, I found a neighborhood market and grabbed some fresh fruit and a bottle of tequila. I'd have a shot and toast Nico before I had to attend the stupid committee meeting for the gala. I made a point to spend at least twenty minutes each day remembering my soulmate and partner in crime. I missed him so much. It seemed as if the pain would never lessen. For so long after his death, every time something interesting happened to me, I'd think, "I can't wait to tell Nico." And then realization that he was gone would set in again. At least *that* no longer happened. Baby steps.

Now I spend twenty minutes each day talking to him as if he was sitting there with me. Call me crazy. I don't care. It was actually what kept me sane after he died.

Back in my hotel room, I took a long shower and then dressed in a white, fluffy robe, and poured a shot of the tequila.

I pulled a chair up to the window and faced the Golden Gate Bridge.

The first time I'd ever heard of Nico had been in San Francisco. He'd scared the shit out of me. We were enemies then. He wanted to take Rose away from me. How strange that he had later become the greatest love of my life.

I always believed the saying in *A Bronx Tale*: We only have three great loves in life. I'd had mine: Bobby. James. Nico.

I was done.

And it was okay.

I didn't need a man in my life. Not anymore.

I had a slight buzz on and part of the bottle was drained when Danny called me.

"I did some digging on your people," he said. "I'll email the reports, but it looks like none of them have had any odd financial fluctuations."

I tried to hide my disappointment.

"I'll keep digging," he said.

A bit later, I was about to get in the shower, when Dante called.

"Yo, I'll be there in an hour," he said.

"Where's this meeting anyway?"

"The restaurant. Skyview."

I already knew that.

"Wear the Versace pantsuit I had sent to you."

"What pantsuit?" I glanced over my shoulder.

"Should be in your closet."

I leaped up. "What the fuck? If I'm going to stay here, nobody better come in my suite when I'm not here. That's bullshit."

And sure enough after I raced into the bedroom and glanced in the closet, I saw a freaking white pantsuit hanging from a hook.

I thought of the weapons I had stashed when I first arrived. I'd used my Aunt Eva's special lined suitcase to bring them from Europe. It had secret compartments and was made with a material that withstood any type of X-ray machine—total spy stuff.

"It's a hotel, Gia."

"Right now, it's my home!"

"Just tell them not to come in, no biggie."

I glared at the pantsuit.

"Gia, be ready. I'll be there at five sharp, and we'll head upstairs."

I gave the offending pantsuit another look.

"White's not my color."

"Yeah, yeah. Whatever. Just wear the pantsuit."

I made a face and hung up. Fuck the pantsuit.

I was admiring myself in the mirror when there was a knock at my door.

I hated to admit it, but as usual, Dante was right.

The white pantsuit looked fucking amazing on me. Who knew?

It fit like a dream. I wore the supple blazer without anything underneath, and it was cut low enough to reveal some skin but no boob. *Excellent.* The flowing pants were perfect with my gold stiletto sandals, and I looped some thick gold chains around my neck. They gleamed against the bronze skin of my chest.

Maybe white *was* my color.

There was another knock.

"Coming!"

I scooped up my bag and headed to the door.

When I flung it open, Dante stood there in a sharp black suit with a black shirt underneath.

"Hello, sailor!" I said enthusiastically, leaning over to kiss him on the cheek. "You look positively edible."

"I'm gay, Gia," he said dryly.

"Whatever," I said. I leaned over and licked his cheek.

"Ew."

"Oh, please," I said. And then I stepped back and twirled. "You done good, D. Real good. It's hard to believe, but you've become even more of a fashion plate since you married Wayne. How much do the two of you spend on clothes anyway?"

"Close to the GDP of a small country, I'd imagine," he said without blinking.

He stepped back to admire me and let out a low whistle.

"Wow. I did nail it. Hit it out of the park. I might quit the restaurant business and start dressing celebrities for kicks."

I mock glared. "No way. You're all mine. I'm your only Dress-Up-Barbie-Bitch. I don't share."

"Thank God you listen to me," he said. "At least most of the time."

"The only reason I'm not wearing my "Fuck Authority" T-shirt is because Rose stole it from me."

The first time we met with my father's companies' board, I wore the shirt. Dante was furious.

Now, we both burst into laughter at the memory and then quickly sobered. I missed that girl.

"What's the news on Rose?" Dante asked, his brows knitting together.

I exhaled and shook my head. "She's alive. She was in Florida recently. She's tapped into her inheritance, so I don't have to worry about her starving to death."

"Well, that's good, isn't it?" Dante asked.

"Yeah. I just miss her."

"She never calls?"

I scoff. "No. Well, she did call Eva. That's how I heard she was in Florida."

Dante reached over and enveloped me in a hug. "She is just working some shit out. It probably hurts too much to be in touch with you right now."

"I don't get it," I said. "I never pressure her in any way. I can't think of anything I did to make her upset with me. I just don't understand."

"She's carving her way in the world, Gia," he said. "That girl has gone through the worst sorts of hell. You didn't do anything wrong. Just give her time. And love her."

"It's impossible not to," I said. "I just can't help but worry about her and miss her."

"Normal."

He glanced at his watch.

"Darn! We've got to scoot," he said.

"You're so cute when you swear."

He rolled his eyes as I locked up behind us.

We stepped into the elevator, and he held up a keycard to the scanner. When he did, a new floor I'd never seen appeared. "Skyview."

"That's magical," I said.

"When we take over, we'll give some people VIP cards to come during certain hours. We can program and issue cards for private events, we can hold high-level, top-secret business meetings. We will offer everything. We'll be booked years ahead of time. It's going to be awesome."

"I love it," I said.

"Now, this meeting is where I'll introduce you to everyone as my colleague. Only a few people knew about our bid to buy the restaurant, so we'll keep it under wraps."

"Fine," I said. Then thought of something. "I hope there's booze during the meeting."

"I doubt it."

"Why not?" I said in a pouty voice. "It's at the restaurant, right? Restaurants have alcohol, right? If I would've known that, I would've ordered drinks from room service before I left. This is lame."

"Gia." His voice sounded weary.

"If I'm going to sit through a yawn-worthy committee meeting, I need some booze," I said. "If I would've thought of it, I would have brought a flask and secretly poured it into my coffee. Come on, Dante. I need something to take the edge off. These types of things bore me to tears."

"What are you, twelve years old?"

"Maybe."

"Fine. You can have a drink. One drink."

"Oh please."

"One. Drink."

I scoffed. "Sure. One drink."

The elevator doors whooshed open, and the first thing I saw was a fully stocked bar across the room. The second thing I saw was James sitting in his wheelchair.

I froze. Dante froze and uttered a slight, surprised, "Oh."

James's eyes met mine, and a huge grin spread across his face. He looked older but not much. His black hair was tinged with gray. Smile lines extended from his eyes. His mahogany skin was flawless otherwise. But his smile was contagious. I could feel the grin spreading across my own face. James! Here. Now. My James. A beautiful woman with strawberry blonde hair stood behind him, holding onto the handles of his wheelchair somewhat possessively. I frowned. Where was his wife?

I'd soon find out.

"Well, I guess this isn't going to be so bad after all," I said and made my way over to James.

8

Charles watched her walk in, the bimbo in the white pantsuit.

He'd heard she was some rich bitch joining the fundraising gala board.

Fresh blood was what the board needed. Literally.

He needed more victims. He needed an easy kill.

She would be perfect.

Then he saw her walking over toward the gimp cop in the wheelchair, and his heart raced. Were they friends?

She leaned down and kissed the cop.

Hmmm. The last thing he wanted was for the cop to have more motivation to solve the murders. If they killed this woman and she was the cop's friend, it might provoke a larger investigation than he wanted.

Even from across the room, he could feel Nicoletta bristling at the intrusion from the brunette. He didn't like that. Nicoletta was with the cop for one reason and one reason only—to make sure the cop didn't suspect him.

Nicoletta turned and met his eyes, and he knew all was well.

Nicoletta fucking loved him. She just tolerated the cop, who wasn't even a real man, anyway, was he?

He'd never asked Nicoletta if they had fucked, because he couldn't bear to hear the answer. Just like she never asked what he did with his dick when they were apart. I mean, obviously, she knew, but it was a forbidden subject.

As he watched, one man after another came up to meet the bitch in the white pantsuit.

He hated her on sight. She was the type of woman who would bust his balls if he said anything flirtatious to her. He could tell. He liked his women soft and feminine like his Nicoletta. She wasn't afraid to be a woman. He could grab her ass and tits all he wanted and she liked it.

He tried to hide his disgust with the other woman, standing there like she fucking owned the place. Bitch. He exhaled as someone came up to him, smiling. He stuck out his hand and responded to the greeting, turning his back on the scene across the room.

He'd ask Nicoletta about the brunette later.

9

As I approached, I could feel the redhead's eyes on me, but I ignored her.

I only had eyes for James. We'd locked eyes. It felt like the rest of the room and the chatter had disappeared, and there was only this bubble with me and James in it.

Walking across the room to him seemed to take an eternity.

And then I was there. In front of him. I leaned down to kiss him on the cheek, and he curled his fingers in the back of my hair and kissed me on the lips. Then he grabbed both of my hands in his.

I'm not gonna lie—sparks flew. It lasted about two seconds, but when I pulled back, my cheeks were on fire.

"Long time no see, sailor."

"Gia Fucking Santella. You are a sight for sore eyes."

His grin was contagious. We just sat there for a few seconds beaming at each other like idiots.

We were still holding hands. His wheelchair was tall enough that I only had to lean over a tiny bit.

The strawberry blonde behind him cleared her throat.

"Oh!" James said. "I'm so sorry. Gia Santella meet Nicoletta Van Cleef."

"Nice to meet you," I said.

"The pleasure is mine," she purred. Her voice was warm, but her eyes were cold as death. She didn't like me. Fine. What else was new.

I'd given up on caring whether other women liked me when I turned eighteen.

"Nicoletta is playing the lead role in *The Death of Engleberg*."

"Impressive," I said with a smile, having no idea if that was the right answer.

She gave a delicate shrug. "It's not my most challenging role, but it's been entertaining so far."

"Great," I said and then turned toward James. The last thing I wanted to do was talk about this schmaltzy opera singer's career.

"What in the hell have you been up to for the past decade," I said.

A shadow passed across his face. That's when I knew.

"Genevieve?" I asked in a small voice.

I saw his Adam's apple bob as he swallowed and looked down.

"I lost her to breast cancer five years ago."

"Oh god," I said and leaned down to hug him. "I'm so sorry, James."

I breathed the words into his ear and he held me tight.

"It devastated me and Janie."

I pulled back and searched his eyes. "That's not fair. I'm so sorry."

I was also thinking, *That's why this strawberry blonde is eyeballing me. She's territorial. She's got her meat hooks into James.*

She wants to make sure I'm not a threat. Which I wasn't. That ship had sailed a long time ago, honey. Me and James were destined to be friends. Even if the chemistry between us was off the fucking charts. It was interesting that with Bobby, the chemistry was good but it was more of a soul connection. With James, it was mostly the undeniable electricity between us. With Nico, it was both.

James choked up telling me about Genevieve, so I gave him a few seconds before asking, "How is your daughter?"

Thank God, his face lit up again. "She's amazing. She just started her freshman year at Davis. She's so beautiful and smart and kind, Gia."

"How could she not be? Look at her mama and papa," I said in a low voice.

Just then, Dante made an announcement for everyone to take a seat.

I looked up and for the first time noticed the room we were in.

The space was beautiful. Stunning. It possibly held the best views of San Francisco in the city. There was a 360-degree view broken up by three doors. One door was the elevator. I wasn't sure what the other two were. Even the bar was set up against a window, the brilliant colors of the liquor bottles reflecting the light behind them.

If you whirled in a circle, you'd see the Golden Gate Bridge, Alcatraz, the Bay Bridge, the South Bay, the Pacific Ocean and up closer, the city below.

"Unfucking believable," I said.

Nicoletta shot me a wide-eyed look. I smirked. Miss Opera Singer was offended by the F-word? Just fucking wait.

We took our seats at a banquet table that lined the window facing the Golden Gate bridge. I sat by Dante. James and Madame Butterfly sat at the other end of the table. An older gentleman sat on one side of me. He was very debonair and distinguished-looking, but he seemed frail.

"Oliver Kingsley Hollingsworth at your service," he said and bowed his lips to my palm.

I raised an eyebrow and then fluttered my eyelashes. "Aren't you the charmer? Giada Valentina Santella."

It was rare for me to whip out my full name, but something about this man and his own pretentious-as-fuck last name demanded it. Then I noticed the man beside him.

"This is Charles Wellington," the older man said.

Charles stuck out his limp hand, and I shook it. He was a looker. He had swooping dark hair, full, voluptuous red lips, and a beak-like nose that only made him seem more aristocratic.

"Charles has the lead role in *The Death of Engleberg*," the older man said and puffed out his chest.

"How lovely," I said. "I just met Miss Von Beef."

Charles furrowed his brow and didn't answer.

Interesting. Maybe the two didn't like one another. That could make some dramatic chemistry on stage. It could be really bad. Or really good.

"Yes, Nicoletta is a good girl," Hollingsworth said.

I didn't smile. What a fucking schmuck. Good girl? An accomplished professional opera singer was not a girl. I was biting my tongue and finally couldn't stand it any longer.

"You must mean 'woman,' my dear Mr. Hollingsworth," I said and plastered a smile on my face.

He guffawed. "Oh, yes. I forget that 'girl' is no longer acceptable. My apologies, Miss Santella. I'm eighty-nine years old, and sometimes it's hard to keep track of how things change. My memory isn't as good as it used to be."

I smiled back—a genuine one this time and dipped my head.

Old fart managed to charm the fuck out of me and defuse my prickly side.

I kind of liked him for it.

"It's definitely a lot to keep track of," I said. "I always try to be aware of my words so I don't offend anybody, and yet, when I had a teenager at home, she'd point out about every other day something I'd been saying for years that was now offensive. It's definitely hard to keep track. I appreciate your open-mindedness to my comment."

"But of course."

The man on the other side of Dante stood up and cleared his throat.

"I think we've all had time to catch up, so I'd like to start the meeting," he said. "As many of you know, I'm Dick Carriger, vice president of the San Francisco Opera Association.

He was a distinguished-looking man with long dark hair in a ponytail and wore a three-piece black suit with a purple tie.

"Before we get started, however, I do want us to take a moment to remember Samuel Glass. He was found dead this morning, as most of you know. The police are investigating."

A murmur ran through the group. I'd nearly forgotten. *Fuck. Oops.*

But there were no gasps of surprise, so I assumed everyone already knew about the man's death. People bowed their heads. I didn't. I didn't know the dude. I noticed that Nicoletta didn't, either. She was staring at Mr. Hollingsworth. It was so strange.

Then Carriger spoke again.

"I'd also like to introduce our newest committee member, Gia Santella."

He gestured at me and I smiled. "She will be taking over Tiana's role as the head of the speaker and entertainment committee now that Tiana is on maternity leave and busy with those two bundles of joy. Welcome."

"Thank you," I said. As soon as everyone looked away, I shot Dante an alarmed look. I already had an assignment? Nice of him to warn me.

"Our first order of business," Carriger said, "should, sadly, be on filling another now-vacant committee head. Would anyone here have time to take on Mr. Glass's responsibilities? I know that's asking a lot, but I think since he'd already organized most of the auction items, it would just be following up. Do we have any volunteers?"

"I can do it," a handsome man with a deep tan said. He met my eyes and I looked away quickly. I was not in the mood.

At that point, I began to tune out the meeting.

It was pretty damn boring. I tried hard to pay attention, but was really only interested in sliding over to the bar and pouring myself a drink. At one point Dante caught my eye, and I jutted my chin toward the bar. He shook his head in exasperation.

There was a short break called, and I walked over, stepped behind the bar, and made myself a tall tequila straight up. I downed it and was back in my seat before the meeting began again.

Finally, what felt like hours later, the meeting was over.

After, while I looked longingly at the bar with all the booze, we said our goodbyes as people filed past where we stood by the elevator.

"It was a pleasure to meet you," Mr. Hollingsworth said. His boy toy, Charles, dipped his head at me but didn't speak. He was a little odd.

People milled around two separate doors that I realized were elevators on opposite sides of the room.

"What's behind the other doors?" I asked Dante.

"Stick around. I'll give you a tour as soon as everyone leaves. One is to the kitchen. One is a stairwell."

"Nice."

"First, let me introduce you to some of the key players. You met Mr. Hollingsworth and Charles."

"Match made in heaven," I said dryly. I thought it was appropriate that Hollingsworth was called by his last name with "mister" and his fuck boy was simply called "Charles."

Dante shot me a warning glance. "Oliver Hollingsworth is one of the richest and most powerful men in San Francisco. I'm sure he has his choice of boy toys," he said in a low voice.

"I get it. But he's a hell of a lot more charming than his boy toy. I figured he could be pickier. Fuck someone with a little more personality."

"Gia!"

"What?"

Then Dante plastered a broad smile on his face.

"Gia, may I introduce you to Mayor Anthony Ferraro."

It was the man with the deep tan. He looked like he spent his spare time getting mani-pedis. He was just a little "too" pretty and groomed, as if his suits could stand up on their own.

We Italians called men like this, "mammones." They were mama's boys who lived at home, sponging off mama's cooking and cleaning until they were in their forties.

I liked my men a little more rugged and independent.

I thought of Ryder, and a surge of lust raced through me. Damn. That was unexpected. I snuck a glance around the room and spotted James. It was probably his fault, as well.

"Don't you think, Miss Santella?"

Shit. The mayor had asked me something. I raised an eyebrow and gave a noncommittal shrug.

Fuck. What had he asked. I looked at Dante, and he didn't seem alarmed so my response must have been okay.

Just then, thank God, someone else walked up and Dante introduced me. At the same time, someone pulled the mayor aside.

"Jackie Fong meet Gia Santella. Jackie is head of the City by the Bay Hospitality Group. Gia and I are business partners."

Jackie Fong had a chic silver bob and a warm smile. She

wore wide-leg silk pants and had layers of wooden beaded necklaces looped around her neck. I liked her instantly.

"Nice to meet you," I said and meant it.

"I'm so glad you are coming on board," Jackie said. "Ever since Tiana left, I've been swimming upstream around here. There's way too much testosterone in this room for my liking," she said and winked. "I'm not talking about you, Dante."

"Hey! Gay men have plenty of testosterone. Trust me."

She ignored him and grasped both of my hands.

"I'm in charge of securing sponsorships for the gala. Let me know if you have any ideas. I'm pretty much set, but a new take on the city and its offerings is always welcome. We tend to approach the same organizations year after year. Sooo boring. We need to reach more businesses owned by women. I'm sick of the old guard being the only ones showcased at this gala. This is the year it's going to be different."

"Of course," I said.

"She's right," Dante said. "Hollingsworth is the last of the old guard on this committee. This is the first year we're shaking it up."

"Thank God, Dante is in more of a leadership role this year. It's changed everything. Let's talk more later, Gia. I have to run," she said, leaning forward and air kissing me. "I have a meeting with the governor. He's in town for the weekend."

And then she was gone.

"She's a force," I said to Dante as we both watched her get into the elevator.

"She used to run a Fortune 500 company. She retired and bought another company—a Silicon Valley startup—but that apparently doesn't keep her busy enough, so she runs the hospitality group now too."

"I like her," I said.

"Me too," he said. "By the way, you were rude to the mayor."

"I was?"

"Yes. You need to be nice to him. He can make our life here as hotel owners miserable if he wants."

"Oh."

Then Dante introduced me to Carl Rosenbloom.

He was head of the San Francisco Chamber of Commerce. He had a slight paunch and thinning hair, but his smile was genuine and his eyes seemed kind behind his wire-rimmed glasses. But as soon as we were introduced, his phone buzzed.

He glanced down at it and then frowned. After that, he wouldn't meet my eyes. He kept looking off past me, over my shoulder. So much so that I actually turned to look if there was something behind me. There wasn't. Just a view of South San Francisco.

"Well, it was nice to meet you."

"Yeah, yeah," he said and then realized what he was saying. "I'm sorry. I'm a little distracted today."

He finally met my eyes. I smiled. I could forgive that. We all have tough days.

"No problem," I said. "Looking forward to working with you in the future."

"Likewise," he said. And then he was gone.

"That was weird," I said.

"Yeah," Dante said and frowned. "He's usually more congenial. I think he must have a lot on his mind. I heard that the chamber of commerce is really getting a lot of heat from people protesting the opera. He's sort of in the hot seat since he's head of the chamber, on this committee, and also CEO of a company that was accused of anti-Semitism a few years back after a Jewish man was fired."

"Oh shit," I said. "No wonder he was distracted. Do you think he's anti-Semitic?"

"No way," Dante said. "He doesn't defend himself publicly, but his wife is Jewish."

"Well, there you have it," I said. "Why doesn't he tell people who accuse him of being anti-Semitic that."

Dante shrugged. "No clue."

"Can we go?"

"Soon. You've met the biggest movers and shakers, but let's introduce you to everyone else just briefly."

"Seriously?" I shot a glance at the bar. "Can't I have a drink?"

"Later," Dante said and then introduced me to everyone else.

Finally, I'd met everyone. I was about to sneak over to the bar while Dante had his back turned when James appeared before me.

Madame Butterfly stood beside him, looking annoyed.

"When are we going to get together?" he said. "I need to know everything. We need to catch up on ten years."

"Definitely," I said. "Give me your phone."

He laughed. He punched in his code and handed it to me. "What are you going to do? Snap me?"

"You have Snap?" I said, referring to Snapchat.

"Hello. I have a seventeen-year-old," he said.

"Yeah," I said. "Rose made me get it too."

"How is Rose?"

I was surprised. "She hasn't kept in touch?"

James had been a father figure to Rose for a long time. Every once in a while, when she was growing up, she'd tell me she'd heard from him. I'd assumed they'd kept in touch.

"We lost touch a few years ago. I figured I was just a pest, so I didn't press the issue when she stopped responding to my texts," he frowned. "Maybe that was the wrong thing to do."

My heart hurt suddenly. Rose was so good at pushing everyone who cared about her away.

"She's had some struggles, James. Nico got Alzheimer's and died."

"I'm so sorry. I didn't even ask about Nico."

"It's okay," I said and meant it. "I lost him many years ago when he got Alzheimer's. I'm just grateful I had as much time with him as I did."

"You two were a formidable couple," James said.

And that right there is why James and I will be able to be friends forever.

It seemed to lighten up Madame Butterfly as well.

"I'm so sorry for your loss," she said, tossing her perfect and silky head of hair.

I just looked at her. *Whatever.*

I turned back toward James and handed him his phone.

"I've added you on Snap," I said. "Check your schedule for the next few days and let me know when we can get together.

"I'm working, so I'll have to check my shifts, but I'll get back to you asap."

"SFPD still?"

"He's a commander," Miss Van Cleef said.

We both ignored her.

Every time she spoke, a flicker of annoyance surged over me. Could I have a goddamn conversation with my old friend without her chiming in.

"Anytime, James. I'm available for breakfast, lunch, or dinner."

The only reason I didn't add "dessert" was because Dante would have kicked me in the shins.

10

After the elevator whooshed shut with James and Madame Butterfly inside, Dante turned to me.

"She's a piece of work."

"I can't believe James would fall for that phony shit," I said.

"Gia, you're not jealous, are you?"

I made a face. "Hardly. She's a cream puff. All fluffy and sweet with no substance."

"Huh," Dante said. He crossed his arms and smirked at me.

"Stop. Show me around already."

The swinging doors to the kitchen opened up to a short flight of stairs. The kitchen was actually on the floor below, which was how the restaurant had its 360-degree views. Impressive. The other door led straight up to the roof where guests could "take in the night air" as Dante said like a freaking character out of a Jane Austen novel.

"There's another stairway from the kitchen to a portion of the rooftop that's blocked off," Dante said. "It's got air conditioning units and so on, but it's actually a better view than the public view."

"Nice."

"Yeah. It's where I go to think sometimes."

"How long have you been thinking of buying this place?"

"Years."

"And it just now came up for sale?"

"Yes."

"This is great. I can't wait to go into business with you again, Dante. We make a damn good team."

He checked his watch. "I'm flying to San Diego to spend the weekend with Wayne. Want to come?"

"I think I better stick around," I said, airily. "After all, I just got home. I have a lot of unpacking and catching up to do."

Dante smirked. "Sure. I heard what you said to James."

"Sorry. Not sorry. We never could resist each other," I said. "I haven't gotten laid for a while. I'm horny. So sue me."

"You're such a dude, Gia," Dante said.

"That's not what James would say."

Dante just rolled his eyes.

We stepped into the elevator. I pushed the button for the lobby.

"I'll walk you out," I said.

Downstairs, when the valet brought Dante's rental car, I grabbed him by the chin and kissed him on the lips.

"I love you, paesano. Give Wayne a kiss for me too."

He hugged me tightly and then whispered in my ear. "I'm so glad you're back home."

"Me too."

I stood and watched his car drive away.

I was about to turn when I felt someone at my side.

"He's pretty amazing, isn't he?"

In surprise, I turned to see the mayor. Was the mayor gay? I was about to tell him that Dante was happily married when I saw the way he was looking at me.

"It's great to have you on board," he said. "We could use fresh blood on the committee."

"Is that what I am?" I said lightly.

He cocked his head. "I can't believe we didn't run into each other when you used to live here."

Unless he liked getting shit-faced at my favorite bar—Anarchy—I doubted we would've crossed paths. But I didn't say that. Instead, I said, "With all due respect, mayor, I don't think we ran in the same circles."

"I spent a lot of time in North Beach during those years. Dante said you did, as well. I also lived in the Tenderloin a few years back."

"Oh," I frowned.

"That surprises you?"

I shrugged. "Yeah. You just don't look like the type to go slumming in the T.L."

"*L'Abito Non Fa il Monaco.*" It translated to "Don't judge a book by its cover" or "Clothes don't make the man."

"So, you're Italian?" I asked.

"Half."

"Nice."

"Nice?" His voice was teasing.

I took another look at him. So his skin wasn't just tanned from trips to Florida every year. Come to think of it, his last name was Italian—Ferraro.

He cleared his throat. "I'm sure North Beach has changed a little since you were last here, but one of my favorite restaurants is still open. Rossetti's Cucina."

"Yeah, that's a good one."

I was getting eager to leave. This small talk was killing me. I wanted to go upstairs and change out of my white suit and into soft jeans and a worn T-shirt.

"I have a reservation for dinner tonight, but my colleague's flight was delayed," he said and paused. *Shit*. He was asking me out. I stared wide-eyed like a deer in the headlights.

"I'd hate to let the reservation go to waste. It usually takes a few weeks to get in.

"Oh."

"I'm asking you to dinner," he said with a smile.

"Oh. Oh!" I said. "Um, sure." My response was lame.

But his smile remained.

"Pick you up at seven? Here?"

"All right," I said and turned to leave.

On the elevator ride up to my room, I was kicking myself. *Fuck*. I was out of shape at turning down dates. He was hot and all.

I mean, I probably wouldn't kick him out of bed, but I'd rather have James. James and I had a rhythm down. No bullshit. No awkward moments. It was pure animal lust. I didn't need to have some new guy in my life who might expect more. Or, God forbid, would want to stay the night and cuddle. No thanks. I was over that.

Plus, I was not interested in going on a date and making small talk. Not to mention, even though I was Italian, I had a strict rule against dating Italian men.

Who needed that macho bullshit?

Fuck. I was trapped. I had to play nice since he was the mayor and Dante had ordered it.

Inside my room, I finally poured the drink I'd been craving all afternoon.

I stripped off the beautiful white suit and hung it carefully in the closet. Standing in my underwear sipping my tequila, I eyed my clothes. What would be appropriate for dinner with the mayor? Fuck if I knew.

I dialed Dante.

"Ugh. The mayor asked me to dinner."

"Oh, poor Gia."

"I have nothing to wear."

"I know just the thing," he said.

Of course, he did.

"Wear your black trousers with that emerald green camisole, and throw your leather blazer over it. Not the Patty Hearst one with the rough, scratched leather—the Gaultier one that looks like it's silk."

"Got it," I said with my phone between my ear and shoulder, as I pawed through my rack of clothes in the closet. "What shoes? What jewelry?"

"Your emerald drop earrings—the monster-size ones that Nico got you for your fifth anniversary."

"Yep. I have those."

"And then on your feet, how about your peep-toe platform black Louboutin's with the stiletto-heel?"

The question in his voice concerned me.

"You sure?"

He was quiet for a minute.

"No. Do closed-toe for tonight. The Jimmy Choo pumps."

"Okay.

"Have fun," he said. "Behave yourself."

"Impossible," I said and hung up.

If only he had advice to stop me from sleeping with the next handsome man who gave me attention…

I needed to get laid asap, or I would do something I would regret.

I texted James.

"Hey, cowboy. When are you free?"

I waited but there was no response.

Damn it.

But a small part of me was glad he didn't respond.

I pretended that what was between me and James was purely

physical, but that was a lie. It wasn't fair to him. He was way more than a sexual partner. I loved James.

I always would. It's just that we could never be together.

Unlike Nico, and even my latest love interest, Ryder, James could never know the things I've done in my life. I could never share that part of myself with him. I wouldn't be able to bear the shame and guilt. I couldn't bear him looking at me with scorn or disappointment.

Thinking this, I texted Ryder.

"San Francisco is really beautiful this time of year," I wrote. "Most of the tourists who came for the summer and found it was cold AF have left. Now the really nice weather begins."

I hit send and waited.

I saw the bubbles showing he was replying. Then the message appeared and made me smile.

"Is that a hint? You want me to book my ticket?"

"I wouldn't complain if you did," I wrote back.

"It wouldn't be until after the first of the year. This new client has me running my ass off day and night. But after New Year's Day, he's heading back to Brazil for the rest of winter, and my job will end."

"But that's so far away," I typed, wondering if the words conveyed the whine in my voice.

"I'd invite you to visit me here, but dude has me at his beck and call. Good news is he ain't cheap."

"What are you doing right now? This second?"

"I just got out of the shower."

Jesus Christ.

I could just picture him, naked in all his glory.

"Do you have a towel around your waist?" I typed and then held my breath.

"Do you want me to have one?" he wrote back.

"Definitely not."

"How about you?"

I set down the phone and tugged off my T-shirt. I wasn't wearing a bra.

I propped the phone on the dresser in my bedroom and then wriggled out of my jeans. Then I lay back and held the phone up above my head so it showed my head, my bare breasts, and the top of my black lace underwear, where I put my other hand.

After I sent the photo, I lay back in the bed, breathing heavy.

My phone dinged. I glanced over.

He had replied with one word: "Damn."

I grabbed my phone, and before I could change my mind typed, "Let me see you. Please."

To my surprise, he sent a short video. So of course I had to send one back.

And then I just said "Fuck it" and Facetimed him.

11

JAMES WAS DRUNK.

Nicoletta kept pouring him drink after drink out of the seeming endless pitcher of margarita she'd made. They were sitting on his deck overlooking the street below. The sun was setting, and he was out of sorts.

Seeing Gia had sent him into a tailspin.

He'd thought that his feelings for her were platonic. He'd thought that after all those blissful years as Genevieve's husband and loving her with all his heart, his feelings for Gia would be gone.

But as soon as he saw her, he knew his feelings for Gia would never die. He would love her in some form forever. But he also knew they could never be together.

Nicoletta hadn't brought it up yet, but he knew it was simply a matter of time.

She wasn't an idiot. She must've felt the electricity between them.

Nicoletta sidled up to him, pressing her breast against his shoulder as she leaned down to fill up his glass once again.

He reached for her hand. "Sit, baby. You've been busy in the kitchen since we got home."

"I like to take care of my man," she said in a sweet voice.

He smiled, instantly feeling guilty for all the thoughts he had about Gia. He didn't deserve Nicoletta. She was all soft and feminine and nurturing. Just what he needed after two years of lonely grieving for Genevieve. Nicoletta didn't ask for much, just his time.

She sat down.

"Honey, you just seem like you have a lot on your mind. Is there anything I can do?"

"I owe you an explanation," he said. "That woman?"

"The pretty brunette?"

Pretty. Gia was sexy, mysterious, gorgeous, but pretty? It seemed as lightweight as saying someone was "nice." But he nodded.

"We were together years ago, and it just shook me to see her in person again."

"Oh," Nicoletta said and looked down. Her lower lip trembled. *Fuck.*

He reached over for her hand. "We didn't work out for a reason."

Nicoletta nodded, not looking up.

"I'm a cop," he slurred. Fuck he was drunk.

"I don't get it," she said.

He rubbed his eyes with the back of his palm.

Maybe he should wait to have this conversation when he was sober. Otherwise, he might say something he regretted or that hurt her feelings. She didn't deserve that. But she did deserve an explanation. And she deserved it now, not later.

"I'm a cop. That means my duty is to enforce the law, right?"

Nicoletta nodded.

"Well, Gia...let's just say she doesn't always follow the law."

"I don't get it," Nicoletta said, frowning.

Of course, she doesn't, James thought. Which is partly why he was with her. She was so confident and arrogant on stage in her role as an opera star, but when it came to being a woman in the real world, she was surprisingly helpless. For some reason, it made him feel more masculine to be able to take care of her. He wanted to protect her and keep her safe.

"Are you saying she breaks the law? Like steals?" Nicoletta asked.

"Worse."

"Worse than stealing?"

He didn't answer.

Nicoletta's eyes widened. "Has she killed someone?"

Dear Lord Jesus. What in the hell was he supposed to say to that. Of course, Gia had killed people. That was entirely the problem. In most cases, it hadn't been her fault. They were self-defense? Or were they? That was the problem. He never really knew 100 percent if all the murders had been necessary. Of course, *Gia* had thought they were necessary. But...

"James?"

He jumped. He'd been lost in thought and hadn't answered her question.

"I'm drunk," he said. "I think I need to go to bed."

He turned and began to wheel himself into the house.

"Oh, honey, I thought we could...you know?" She gave him a sexy grin.

He smiled back. "I'm so drunk. How many of those did you pour me?"

She shrugged. "I feel fine."

He blinked.

In the bedroom, he hauled himself out of his wheelchair and into the bed. The room was spinning.

Nicoletta climbed on top of him and began to undo his pants. He grinned at her but then gently pushed her away.

He could barely keep his eyes open. What was going on?

The next thing he knew, the covers were being pulled up to his chin, and he felt Nicoletta's soft, silky hair brush his face as she leaned down and kissed his forehead.

"Sweet dreams, James."

12

He was slouched in his favorite armchair at Nicoletta's Richmond District apartment sipping cheap whisky.

It was fine, he told himself. Soon, he would only drink top shelf. This was temporary.

Everything was going as planned.

Then the door opened. It was Nicoletta, home from that cop's house. She'd promised she'd be back before midnight. She'd come through. He wondered how she'd talked the cop into letting her leave?

She wore a filmy beige dress. He could see her huge nipples through it.

"Oh, baby, I missed you so much," Nicoletta said, walking in and stretching languorously, her large breasts thrusting against the fabric of her dress. "Seeing you today across the room and not being able to kiss you and hold you killed me. I got James drunk so I could come home early."

"I'm so glad you did," he said. "It won't be much longer. And then we will be away from this cold, gray city and can do whatever the hell we want whenever we want."

He walked over and poured them both drinks.

He handed one to her and downed his. Then he plopped back in the chair, spreading his legs, watching her through slit eyes.

"I can't wait, baby," she said in her little girl voice. She stood in the middle of the room holding her glass. She was so damn sexy. She took a small sip of her drink and made a face. He laughed.

"Put it down."

She did, then stood there, waiting, compliant as always. Uncertain. Even though he would do anything she wanted, she always wanted him to boss her around. She made him feel like a true man. Nobody had ever made him feel like Nicoletta did, not even the love of his life, his dear departed wife. In Nicoletta's eyes, he was powerful and manly. She loved when he was in charge. She liked being bossed around. And yet, she was still a strong woman in her own right.

"Come here," he said in a gruff voice.

She came and stood before him. She was trembling. He loved that. It made him feel like he was debauching her, even though they'd fucked hundreds of times. That was what was so magical about her—fucking her was always fresh and new. It never, ever got old. He could imagine them old and gray, still horny as fuck for one another.

He smiled and reached for her, bending down to lift the hem of her dress and pull it entirely over her head.

"Good girl."

He'd told her before to never ever show up at his place with underwear on. He liked imagining her walking around naked underneath her dresses while he was the only one who knew. It turned him on.

He dipped his fingers in his whiskey and rubbed her nipples. She threw her head back and moaned.

He reached down and found her sopping wet. She was

always wet, but this was something else. She moaned louder as he touched her.

He watched her eyes start to close in ecstasy.

"I found our next victim," he said, and her eyes snapped open. "I think it should be Jackie Fong. That hospitality group bitch."

"I have an even better idea," she said.

He grabbed her and threw her over his shoulder, carrying her over to the bed. He set her down on the edge and dipped his head between her legs.

She lifted his head. "Don't you want to hear it?"

"Later," he said, pulling himself up on top of her.

"This is really good. You'll like this," she said.

"I said, 'later,'" he growled and reached up and pinched her nipple so hard it brought tears to her eyes.

Then he yanked off his pants and fucked her so hard that the entire bed felt as if it were going to break in two.

She came before he did. He knew her better than she knew herself. He knew when she needed it soft and sensuous and when she needed it hard and fast.

When he was done, he rolled over and flopped on his back.

"So, baby doll, I'm ready to listen now. What's your plan? You think we let Fong live and take out someone else? Maybe that brunette cunt."

Nicoletta sat up on one elbow, her eyes sparkling.

"Oooh, you're so clever. You knew that's who I was thinking about, but I have a twist. You said Marshall can make anyone we want the killer, right? With that technology?"

"Yeah," Charles said sitting up.

"She's not another victim. She's the killer."

He sat up. "What? Didn't you say she was the cop's ex?"

He never called James by name. That would give the guy a dignity he didn't deserve. However, he did manage to stop himself from calling him the "gimp cop"; that was just how he thought of the guy in his own head. Even Nicoletta would look down on him for that, and she wasn't one to worry about being politically correct.

"Like I said," Nicoletta said, sitting up and fluffing her hair. "I got him drunk—really drunk—and asked about her. He basically told me that the reason they didn't work out is because she did illegal stuff."

He frowned. "Like what? Fraud? Shoplifting?"

"Murder."

Nicoletta said the word and gave him a triumphant smile.

His eyes widened.

"Yep, he basically told me she was a killer.

"No fucking way."

He jumped up.

"This is fucking perfect," he said. He threw his hand in the air, fist pumping.

"I know!" she said and stood on the edge of the bed, bouncing lightly up and down.

He looked up at her naked curves and smiled.

"You are not only the most beautiful woman in the world, but you are also the smartest."

She grinned and then ran her hands over her boobs, slowly and sensually.

To his surprise, he felt some movement down there. It usually took a little longer to recharge, but plotting murder turned him on as much as Nicoletta's centerfold body.

"Come show me how much you appreciate me," she said. "I'm still horny."

He didn't have to be asked twice.

13

After hanging up with Ryder, I laughed to myself. We were like goddamn teenagers.

But I felt better. I'd released some of my pent-up sexual frustration and felt like I could go to dinner with the mayor without attacking him just because he was halfway good-looking.

When I got out of the shower, I saw Ryder had texted me.

"Let's do that again real soon."

"You bet."

I was five minutes late getting downstairs to meet the mayor. I couldn't stop thinking about him as "the mayor" even though I knew his name. Fucking Italian mama's boy.

He was standing just outside the lobby doors, chatting with the valet. They were in such an animated conversation I stood there for a few seconds.

The mayor was talking about some musician he'd just seen live, and the kid with the spiky hair was impressed.

"Damn," the valet said with a low whistle. "I'm green with envy."

"Yeah," the mayor said. "I'm not going to lie. It was cool."

Then they noticed me and the mayor looked up with such a

big smile, I felt like my eyes magically transformed into emoji heart eyes. He *was* cute.

What woman wouldn't want a guy to look at her and smile like that.

"Ready?" he asked.

"Let's do this."

He held my door open as I got into his low-slung, black Acura NSX. The mayor's salary must not be that bad.

Ten minutes later, we were in North Beach. He valet parked the car, and we dipped inside the dark and moody restaurant. The walls were covered in red velvet wallpaper adorned with black and white signed photos of celebrities. We sat under a signed picture of Frank Sinatra in a back, corner booth.

"This is my favorite table," he said. We sat with our backs to the wall of the semi-circular booth, giving us a view of the entire restaurant.

"You a former cop?"

He laughed. "No. Politicians need to see whose coming for a different sort of attack. Usually I'm ducking a verbal barrage instead of bullets."

"Nice," I said, sipping the martini I'd ordered. "Don't suppose you ever woke to a horse's head in bed?"

"No, thank God, but I have woken to find a dead animal on my front steps."

"Ew," I said and made a face.

"Yeah. I moved right after that."

"I don't blame you," I said. "What was that all about?"

"I voted against a motion to build a luxury hotel in North Beach," he said and pointed. "Right there. Next to Columbus Square."

"Ouch," I said. "You anti-hotel?"

He laughed. "Dante already told me about your bid to buy the hotel. I don't have a problem with it. But you might find some people on the planning commission who don't like the idea of the helipad."

I squinted my eyes. "Dante told you all that?"

He shrugged. "We're old friends."

"Old friends?" I said in a skeptical voice.

"Well, not old like you guys. But maybe ten years or so. We worked on the same homeless commission back in the day."

"Huh." *Ten years ago?*

"That okay?"

"Sure."

Inside, I was thinking that sonofabitch didn't tell me he was such great pals with Mr. Mayor. He was holding out on me. Was this date a set up? Probably. Fuck me.

"What's wrong?" Mayor McCheese asked.

"Did Dante make you ask me out?"

He practically spit out his water and burst into laughter.

"What? Like I felt sorry for you."

I smiled and shrugged.

"Actually, to be perfectly honest, he told me to back off," he said.

I nearly spit out *my* water.

The mayor held up his hand. "Let me explain," he said. "He called me this afternoon and said if I didn't treat you like a queen, he was going to bitch-slap me."

I sighed. "That sounds like Dante."

"I mean, I've had people threaten to kick my ass before, but nobody has ever threatened to bitch-slap me, so I'm going to listen to him."

I gave a wry grin. The guy was cute and funny.

"I'm not feeling very queenlike right now," I said. "Maybe if you order me another drink...?"

He stood and was at the bar across the room before I finished the sentence. I laughed. I liked him.

People stopped to watch him. He was that sort of personality. His presence took over a room.

He was charismatic and funny and kind. He was one of the most powerful men in the city, and yet he didn't take himself too seriously. He was back with martinis before I could reapply my lipstick.

"Thank you, kind sir."

"The jester at your service, my lady."

"Oh, you are hardly the jester," I said.

He met my eyes over the crystal glass of water he was sipping from and raised an eyebrow.

"Don't worry," I said. "You're not the jester, but it's going to take me time to figure out just who you are."

"Oh, do take your time," he said. "I mean this isn't something to be taken lightly—telling me who I am."

We both laughed.

We ate lobster ravioli in a creamy lobster sauce followed by tiramisu.

"Tell me about working with Dante?" I said over dessert.

"Only if you tell me about Ethel's Place?" he said.

My cheeks grew hot.

Ethel's Place was my passion project. Shortly after I'd inherited my father's company, I started the nonprofit to help get homeless people on their feet. We built commercial and residential buildings in various cities across the country. The homeless people would move into apartments above the street-level businesses and worked in the small shops on the ground level, which included markets and florists and bookstores. They had a set amount of time to get on their feet before they had to move out so someone else could move in.

The mayor listened attentively. "I knew about their success, but I never heard why you decided to create the nonprofit."

I told him about my homeless friend, Ethel, who had died helping me. She had been killed in retaliation for my actions.

"Whoa," the mayor said when I was done. "That's pretty heavy."

"Why do you have a soft spot for the homeless?" I asked.

He told me how he'd turned an old Cal Trans parking lot into a permanent homeless camp.

By the time he was done, it was late.

The lighting was low, the music was bluesy, and the food was rich and filling. I felt sleepy and warm and satiated and had enjoyed myself enormously.

But we stayed and talked even longer. He told me about his rise to power. He earned it. He worked his way through college and then volunteered the Peace Corps before working for both the Obama campaign and the McCain campaign.

"Checking out both sides?"

"I believe in both sides."

"Impossible."

"But true."

Hmmm. I was a little suspicious, but I let it go.

"You ready to tell me who I am?" he said. "Besides the jester?"

I put my finger to my chin in mock thought.

"After hearing your path in politics, I could say you are Switzerland, but that's a little too pat. You're more than that."

"Oh really?"

"You aren't the jester. You aren't the king—the king is too stodgy and set in his ways. You aren't the prince, either. Princes can be whiny babies like Luke Skywalker. You're a little like Han Solo—sort of rebellious but sexy."

"Sexy?" he said and wiggled his eyebrows.

"Oh yeah," I said, nodding. "So, I think you would probably be Sir Lancelot."

"We've gone from Star Wars to King Arthur in one conversation."

I shrugged. "You don't like Lancelot?"

"Sure, I like Lancelot."

"Wait!" I said so loudly he jumped. "You're fucking Robin Hood!"

"What?"

"Yeah. That's who you are. Case closed. You can't argue."

He laughed so loud that people turned to look. But I noticed that everyone who turned smiled. The dude was loved by everyone.

"This was really nice," I said as he held out his hand to help me up from the booth.

"Yeah," he said and frowned slightly. "I don't remember the last time I've enjoyed myself so much. Thank you."

"Do you want to go dancing in the Castro?" he asked. "It's only midnight."

I yawned. "Can I take a raincheck? I'm still on Sumatra time."

"Of course."

He pulled in front of the hotel, and there was an awkward moment when the valet ran over to open his door. He looked at me, and I gave him a sad smile and shook my head.

"Goodnight," I said and leaned over to kiss his cheek. "I had a great time."

He nodded and then I was gone before he could say anything else.

Upstairs, I stripped off my clothes and collapsed into bed, staring up at the velvet night sky. It was a clear night in San Francisco, and I could see the stars and a sliver of the moon.

Life was good.

I thought about the mayor. He was sweet. And not my type. But I'd still had a good time. I hoped we could be friends. I thought of Ryder and smiled. *He* was my type. Then I thought of James. He was off the hook for a while. I needed to resist having sex with him at all costs. It would open up some deep wounds I didn't need to deal with right then. Like I had for years, I'd continue to love him at a distance.

But then, after I crawled into bed, my phone dinged. A text from James.

"Five tomorrow?" Followed by his address.

Fuck. So much for my pure thoughts about loving him from afar.

Because I knew that as soon as we were alone together within a mile of a bed it was game over.

14

James picked up the phone on his desk and then set it back down.

His head hurt something fierce.

Last night was the first time he'd been drunk since Genevieve died.

The night of her funeral, he'd gotten smashed. His daughter found him passed out on the kitchen floor the next morning. He'd been so ashamed. He'd vowed to never drink too much again. And he hadn't. Until last night.

Seeing Gia and feeling all the feels for her had done it.

It hadn't helped that Nicoletta had kept refilling his glass.

Come to think of it, that was pretty strange. She usually encouraged him to stop at two drinks, but last night, she just kept refilling his glass. He wondered if it was because she sensed how he was feeling about Gia.

He wondered if it was some sort of revenge. But that didn't make sense. How could her revenge be getting him drunk? Unless she was secretly angry at him and wanted him to pass out so she could leave without making love to him or staying the night.

Nah. She didn't have a conniving bone in her body. He was imagining things. She was just being her usual nurturing self. She probably saw he was hurting and confused and was giving him what he actually really wanted—more booze.

He shook out two more aspirin and downed them without water before he turned back to the stack of reports on his desk. He sighed.

Moving up in the cop world meant more paperwork and less time on the street. If he'd only known.

His phone rang, and he scooped it up.

"Lieutenant?"

"Speaking."

"This is Sergeant Ernst. You told me to call you if there were any crimes I thought you might be interested in?"

He closed his eyes thinking *Spit it out, son.*

"Yes?"

"In particular, anything that might be related to the protests at the opera house...?"

"Go on," he said impatiently. Did someone else throw something on one of the actors? He would have heard about it from Nicoletta.

"We just found a DOA, and it looks like it might be Carl Rosenbloom."

"Jesus," James said. "What time was the call?"

"O five hundred."

He glanced at his watch. Less than twenty minutes ago. *Good.*

"Text me the location I'm on my way."

In his unmarked sedan, James raced through the streets of San Francisco. This was bad.

This marked the second murder of someone on the gala fundraising board in two days. It was not a coincidence. He would need to warn the board members. He would also need to warn Gia.

Just thinking her name made him feel on edge.

Why did she have such a powerful effect on him? They were terrible for one another.

They'd tried and tried again.

It would never work.

And yet, she was suddenly all he could think about.

God damn it.

Why did she have to come back into town? Why couldn't she leave him alone and stay far away in a distant country where he didn't have to see her and smell her and feel her cheek brush against his?

The address took him to a residential neighborhood.

A two-block area was marked off with yellow crime scene tape. Neighbors lined the tape, curious.

As he pulled up to the scene, the rookie cop recognized him and lifted the tape allowing his vehicle to glide underneath. A few squads were parked in a semi-circle to hide the body from onlookers.

He parked and was greeted by his homicide lieutenant.

"Identification confirms its Carl Rosenbloom."

James nodded. He bit his tongue but inside he was thinking, *Motherfucker.*

He called the chief.

"Commander?"

"We're dealing with a serial killer, sir," he said. "This is the second member of the opera fundraising board to be found dead in as many days."

"Jesus. Are you at the scene?"

"Yes, sir."

"Call me when you're done. We'll meet this afternoon and form a task force. We need to get ahead of this before the media gets wind."

James glanced at the people behind the crime scene tape. No

TV crews, but he recognized a young man, slouched to one side, wearing expensive sneakers, a hoodie, and Elvis Costello glasses. It was that scrappy, new newspaper reporter for the Daily. The kid had recently graduated from Berkeley and was working the crime beat. One of the first things he did was stalk James with calls and emails until James had let him come into the precincts and introduce himself. Daniel Quan. James admired the kid's ambition, but that didn't mean the little punk wasn't going to be a royal pain in the ass. Especially on a case like this.

"That might be a problem," James said into his phone, keeping an eye on Quan who had begun talking to a woman with red-rimmed eyes. "I'm off to do damage control right now."

But by the time James sent an officer over to the woman, Quan closed his notebook with a smug thump. *Fuck.* He'd gotten her.

The woman was Rosenbloom's daughter. Soon they had her in the back of a squad, away from prying eyes and pesky reporters, but James saw by the way Quan took off on his little scooter, that the kid had figured out who the victim was and the significance.

Damn it to hell.

By the time James made it back to the station, news had spread: Someone was killing members of the opera fundraising gala board.

When James rolled into his office, his secretary, Josh, rolled his eyes.

"Did you see the news crews out front?"

"I'm sure the orbiting satellites saw them too."

"You've got exactly three billion messages from reporters, including the New York Times reporters and Associated Press.

James shook his head. It was already a national story. This was going to be a major problem.

But then the day got even worse.

When he rolled into the conference room, the chief was sitting there with the district attorney, Mark Nolan.

"A witness just came forward. We have a suspect."

"Fantastic," he said and pulled up a chair. "Who's our guy?"

"It's not a guy. It's a woman," the DA said. "Her name is Gia Santella."

15

THERE WAS SOMETHING ABOUT GIA SANTELLA THAT WAS irresistible, Charles thought.

And he was disturbed by it.

Sitting in his favorite armchair smoking a cigar while a silky-wigged head bobbed between his legs, he tried to analyze what it was. The fading sunset over the bay lit up the room in a reddish-gold color.

Thinking of her had made him hard as a rock. Granted, she had a smoldering sexuality that made every man from eighteen to one hundred horny, but it was more than that.

But what was it?

He looked down at the dark head between his legs and gave a small groan.

Having Nicoletta dress up like Gia Santella was hot. It turned him on.

When he got to her place, he made her put on the dark wig and the black leather pants.

Her soft, warm mouth raised, and her eyes met his.

"Like this, baby?" she said, caressing him with both hands.

He shook his head. "You know what I want."

She laughed. "I know. Just teasing."

He forced her head down and thrust forward. His cock was so hard.

He was about to explode. He tried to keep his thoughts on Gia, though.

She was like a fascinating puzzle he was in the midst of solving.

Maybe part of what made her so attractive was that she seemed to do what she wanted to do when she wanted to do it.

The unspoken rule at the committee meeting was that nobody drink anything except water and coffee, but she walked right over behind the bar and poured herself a drink.

The gall! A few eyebrows had been raised. Nicoletta made a face of disapproval. But he couldn't stop staring, waiting to see what she would do next.

He'd seldom met a woman who really didn't seem to care what everyone else thought of her. After the meeting, she barely paid attention to the rich and powerful men fawning over her. In fact, it was as if she barely noticed them.

When he was in front of her, she was polite, but seemed unimpressed.

It wasn't something he'd ever experienced before.

Usually women simpered over him.

Like the woman between his legs. She thought she was in control with his cock in her mouth, but he controlled it all. She just didn't know it yet.

He knew she would do anything for him. She didn't have to say it. He could feel it.

And why not? She saw the way other women looked at him, and it made her insanely jealous. She would die before she admitted it, though.

But it made sense.

After all, he was the whole package: handsome, rich, powerful, talented.... What else could a woman want? He could smile at a woman in the right environment, and an hour later she'd want him to be the father of her children.

It had been like that his entire life. And even from an early age, he knew that it was where his power lay. His mother had doted on him and told him that he was so handsome and so talented and smart and wonderful that he could have the world eating out of his palm.

He'd never doubted it for a second.

And his mother had been right. He had become even more powerful as he grew older. He knew just how to manipulate people—women and men—to get what he wanted.

He was unstoppable. And right then, he was at the height of his power.

But he wasn't through yet. He had some ways more to go before he could sit back and revel in his power and wealth. It wouldn't be long.

So why had meeting that bitch today threw off his game so much? He hated that when Gia Santella had looked at him, he'd felt strangely diminished, as if when it came to him he was like a dime a dozen.

He didn't like it.

Not one bit.

Nicoletta drew back and her huge eyes met his.

"More, baby?"

"Don't fucking think about stopping," he said, his breath raspy with lust. "Seeing that video of you killing Rosenbloom turns me the fuck on."

"It wasn't me, silly. I just pointed the gun."

Like he didn't know that. Marshall's video skills were outstanding.

She gave a knowing smirk and licked her lips before her head dipped back down.

He put his large palms on the back of her head, pushing her mouth on him until he was as deep as he'd ever been.

His thoughts briefly turned analytical as he got back into the rhythm of her mouth. Then with a start, he realized that everything had worked out perfectly.

The more he thought about it, the more he realized that meeting Gia had been his destiny. Her appearance had solved the biggest one of his problems—finding a fall guy. Nicoletta was right. Gia Santella would be the fall woman. His problem had been solved so easily. When her gaze had flickered over him and dismissed him, she had no idea that she'd made a fatal mistake.

His eyes closed as the head bobbing between his legs brought him nearly to a climax.

He leaned back with a smile on his face that turned to a grimace of intense pleasure. He was almost there. He was nearly at the ultimate release.

Thinking of Gia Santella had aroused him.

"Yes," he moaned. Yes, he would show her that he was something special and that his attention should not be dismissed.

He would call her and invite her to a meeting. A deadly meeting.

If she wasn't already in prison for murder. The wheels had been set in motion.

His excitement grew. He gripped the silky head hard and thrust his hips upward. As he erupted into an incredibly intense orgasm, his last thoughts were that Gia Santella would pay for her dismissive behavior.

And pay dearly.

16

"Gia, where were you last night?"

It was James. I was scrutinizing the financial numbers Dante had sent me trying to figure out who could have embezzled the money from the hotel.

"Huh? Last night?"

"Yeah. Where were you last night?"

I rolled my eyes He must have heard about my date with the mayor. Was he jealous?

"In bed." I wasn't going to make it easy for him. "Why?"

"There's a problem."

"What's that?"

"Carl Rosenbloom has been murdered."

"Oh, my god," I said. I didn't know the dude besides our brief meeting where his slimy lips slobbered on my palm, but his murder meant another gala board member dead. "What the hell is going on?"

"We have a witness who saw you talking to him a few minutes before he was murdered."

"Impossible," I said and scoffed.

"Where were you yesterday, say, about one in the morning."

"I was in my hotel room. In bed." *Having phone sex.*

"Were you anywhere before that? With anyone?"

"Yeah," I said. "Before that I went to dinner with the mayor at Rossetti's. Why?"

I could almost feel his jealousy through the phone line. Oh well.

"Did he come up to your room with you after dinner?"

"Is this police business or are you just jealous?" I asked.

"Were you alone?" James repeated, clearly irritated.

I laughed. "Sort of."

"What does that mean?"

Jesus Christ, did he need me to spell it out?

"I was alone, but I was on the phone with someone."

"Huh," he said dryly.

He had no right to act that way. He had no claim to me.

"I'm looking for an alibi for you Gia."

"What the fuck?"

"Just answer me and I'll explain."

"Fine. I was on Facetime. In my bed. Naked. Having phone sex." There, nosy.

"Jesus."

"You fucking asked."

He exhaled. "You're right, I did."

"Why? Where were you? With Madame Butterfly?"

"I'm not a suspect," he said, not answering the question.

"Wait? I'm a suspect?"

"Maybe."

"That makes no fucking sense," I said.

He kept talking. "So, the mayor will verify you were in your hotel room during those hours, right?"

"It wasn't the mayor."

"Whatever. Will that person vouch for you?"

"Uh, yeah. Duh. Obviously, whoever thought they saw me was mistaken."

"Obviously," he said. "Can I get the name and number of the person you were speaking to on the phone?"

I reeled off Ryder's name and number.

"Ryder, huh?"

"Yep."

He hung up without saying goodbye.

What the fuck? He had no right to be jealous. Jesus. And how in the fuckity fuck could I possibly be a murder suspect.

I immediately called Dante and told him about Rosenbloom's murder.

"Apparently, I'm a suspect," I said.

"That makes no sense."

"Tell me about it."

Then I told him what James had said. A witness had seen me.

Just then I got a text from James.

"Hold on," I told Dante and pulled it up.

It was a still shot from video surveillance.

Holy shit. It was a woman talking to Rosenbloom. The image was from behind.

And she looked like me. As much as a woman who dressed in leather pants, a hoodie, and dark sunglasses could look like me. The photo was grainy, but even I thought it looked like me. Even the handbag was the same as the one I had on a chair in the corner—a not-easy-to-find charcoal gray suede Balenciaga bag.

Someone was fucking with me. And hard.

"Dante," I said. "I'm sending you a picture James just sent me."

I waited until he looked at it.

"Gia, that's you, right? Talking to Carl Rosenbloom?"

"Nope. When that picture was taken, I was having phone sex with Ryder."

"Spare me the details."

"You asked."

"Not really."

"The point is, someone is fucking dressing up like me and killing people."

There; I said it.

"That makes no sense."

"Tell me about it," I said, turning to look at my ass in the mirror. It was still shapely even though I'd slacked on my workouts. It was fine, though.

"What are you doing?" Dante asked.

"Why?"

"You seem distracted and not very upset that someone is trying to pin two murders on you."

"*Two?*"

He sighed. "I didn't want to say anything, but James called me earlier and asked what day and time you got into town. I didn't realize why until just now."

"That bastard," I said.

"He's just doing his job."

"I was kidding."

"What I don't get is how she could get that particular Balenciaga bag that quickly? Those aren't easy to find, and whoever it is must've seen yours at the board meeting."

Of course, Dante would notice that detail.

"So, let's narrow it down to the women who were there," I said. "Easy, right?"

"It could be a man who saw you and decided to make you the fall guy," Dante said. "A woman probably wouldn't have been able to take down Rosenbloom and beat him like he was beaten. No offense."

"None taken. But I could've done that and I'm a woman."

"Gia! If you're phone is tapped, you just basically said you could've killed him."

"Not exactly. Plus, my phone isn't tapped."

"Listen, my attorney is calling. I'm going to fill him in, and he's going to give you a call. I think you need a lawyer."

"I doubt it."

"Don't argue."

And then he hung up.

Fuck. If Dante thought I needed an attorney, that worried me, even though part of me doubted anyone could pin a murder on me. They could make me a suspect, but there was no way they'd be able to plant enough evidence for an arrest.

Or could they?

17

JAMES SHOOK HIS HEAD.

It wasn't possible.

Gia wasn't an angel, but she sure as hell wasn't a serial killer, either.

But that photo?

The only connection between the two murders was that the victims both served on the gala fundraising committee.

"What's the motive?" he asked the chief.

"That's your job to find out."

"We can't place her at Glass's death."

The chief shrugged. "But you said yourself she'd just arrived in town that morning."

James bit his lip. "True."

"Figure it out. That's why you get the big bucks around here, Commander. Put your best detectives on it."

"There's something you should know," James said, exhaling loudly.

"I think I know what you're going to say."

"You do?"

"Tish spilled the beans earlier. The suspect is your ex."

"Jesus," James said. "This place is like a coffee klatch."

The chief picked up the folders and stood. "After all these years here, and you act surprised?"

"She didn't do it, Chief."

He turned and raised an eyebrow above his wire-rimmed eyeglasses. "Are you going to be able to be objective on this one? The only reason I'm not yanking you off this case is because I'm hoping you might be able to get her to turn herself in if she's really the killer. I trust you, James."

This was bad. He watched the video again. The camera was across the street and down the block some. It showed only a brief glimpse of the two talking. The woman walked up to the man. They spoke for a few seconds and then moved off camera.

The footage was grainy. You couldn't see her face or profile, but it sure as hell looked like Gia. If only there was a better video —something closer.

James knew it was useless to ask if any other cameras were in the area. The chief was nothing if not thorough.

The chief had also said something about a witness.

James picked up his phone.

"Who was the wit?"

"A homeless guy. Said he knew Gia personally and this was her."

James swore. Gia had always made a point to become friends with the homeless people in the city. This was bad.

"We have a name?"

He heard the rustling of papers. "Warren. We brought him in and showed him some mugs. He picked Gia out. We gave him a ride to the Rustic Diner. Smith gave him some money for breakfast."

James looked at his watch. "How long ago?"

"Twenty?"

James hung up and grabbed his blazer and the keys to his modified Crown Victoria.

The diner was packed. He double-parked in front of the diner and put on the strobe lights so nobody would tow it. After a quick glance inside the restaurant, James headed down the sidewalk as quickly as he could in his wheelchair. Warren would probably be heading back to his neighborhood. Sure enough, two blocks away James saw him, carrying a white Styrofoam container.

James wheeled over to him.

"Warren, my man," he said and gave a huge grin.

The homeless man clutched the container close.

"Hey, I'm sorry to bother you, but I had a quick question for you."

The man frowned, his grizzly, stubbly face scrunching up. "Heh?"

"You know Gia Santella, right?"

The man grinned. "I've known that girl for ages."

"So you saw her last night?"

His face wrinkled. "I think. I was a little tired."

"Yeah?" James asked, making his wheelchair keep up with the man.

"She walk past you or something?"

"Yeah. I was sitting there and she walked right past."

"Didn't say hi?"

Warren worked his lip a little. "Nah."

"That's not really like Gia, is it?"

He shook his head. "It's been a long time. Maybe she didn't recognize me or something."

"Does Gia only say hi to the guys on the streets she knows?"

"Old Gia said hi to everyone but, you know, we all getting old. Maybe she tired of saying hi all the time."

"Huh," James said. He stopped and was about to leave.

"Hey, man I'm heading back to the TL Want a ride?"

Warren looked at him sideways and shook his head. "I'm good. I'm good."

"Okay. Well, thanks for your time."

James was about to leave when Warren cleared his throat. "The cops had me in this morning, and I said I saw Gia. Do you think I got her in trouble? They seemed real happy when I pointed to her picture, you know."

"I think you just need to make sure you are absolutely 100 percent sure you saw her. That's all. You 100 percent sure?"

Warren shook his head. "I dunno. Maybe? I mean it was dark. I'd just had some of my bedtime medicine if you know what I mean?"

He'd been drunk.

"It sure looked like her. I mean, how many broads walk around in a leather pants, sunglasses at night, and high heels."

"High heels?"

"Yeah. I mean, I was sitting on the ground, and they were some tall-ass heels, you know. The kind I don't know how girls walk in."

"Have you seen Gia in heels before?"

He shrugged.

"Did the cops tell you to come back?"

"They gave me a card," he patted his jacket.

"It's good. I don't need to see it."

"They tole me I might hafta come back and tell someone I saw her."

"Okay," James said. "You sure you don't want a ride."

"I'm good, man. I'm good."

James left, wheeling back to his car.

He was glad he'd tracked Warren down. Dude had been drunk the night before and hadn't seen Gia for years. When the detectives hauled him in and showed him pictures, of course he would point to the one of Gia. She was the only one he knew.

James was pretty sure that, as a witness, Warren would be tossed out of court on his ass.

But that wasn't the problem. The problem was the video surveillance.

The heels were interesting, though. Gia was street-smart. She wouldn't show up in a shitty neighborhood to kill someone wearing high heels. It didn't fit.

The call asking Rosenbloom to meet at that corner meant it wasn't a spur of the moment, crime-of-passion, either. It was premeditated.

As far as he was concerned, Gia wasn't a viable suspect.

But even so, the evidence was mounting. It didn't look good.

18

SITTING IN THE DARK WITH THE BLUE LIGHT FROM THE OPEN laptop illuminating his face, Charles glanced over at the closed door.

There wasn't a sound.

He'd snuck out of bed and into the kitchen. Only when he knew he hadn't been detected did he open his laptop.

The email he'd been waiting for was at the top of his inbox.

He clicked on it, and as he read, his heart began to race.

He heard a sound from the other room and quickly slammed the laptop shut. But then he realized it was just the old house creaking.

Opening the computer back up, he stuck in his earbuds and opened the email attachments.

There was Gia Fucking Santella. Ten photos and three videos.

The guy on the dark web had been able to find the pictures and videos.

He clicked on the photos first, saving the best for last.

They were just what his man needed: close ups, full-body shots, candid pictures, and professional headshots. Then he clicked on the videos. Perfect. Seated. Speaking. Walking. From the front and behind. Bingo.

They were perfect.

Obviously, she wasn't concerned with the surveillance cameras outside the hotel or on the streets or even in the meeting rooms. Up until then, she'd had no reason to be.

Big fucking mistake. A fatal mistake for sure.

She had been so careful about everything else.

Information on her was scarce. She'd done a good job concealing her movements and her background.

But not careful enough.

He opened the background report and was astonished. Mother fucker. It was incredible. He just couldn't lose. Everything he touched turned to gold. Her history and background made his plan rock solid.

Nicoletta was right. Gia was a stone-cold killer.

It could not have worked out better.

She'd killed people.

And gotten away with it, but still.

His heart raced.

It wouldn't be long.

Everything was falling into place beautifully.

Soon he would be with Nicoletta forever and they would be wealthy beyond their wildest dreams.

Nicoletta had been perfect.

The handbag was the final touch.

"Just dumb lucky, honey," she told him.

"You don't have to kill him," he'd told her. "Just talk to him and touch his arm. Then walk with him over to the lot. I'll handle the rest."

He, of course, hadn't gotten his hands dirty. He'd paid for the beating and then when Rosenbloom was down on the ground, he'd stood over him and pulled the trigger. Marshall had tapped into the cameras on the street, and they'd determined that no camera angles reached the lot. They were safe that way.

He sent the photos and video to Marshall.

Marshall immediately replied. "These will work."

He wrote back. "How long?"

"Give me a few days."

And now that he had video footage of Gia, they could not go wrong.

He figured after one or two more murders at the most, the stage would be set for the final, most important murder.

He stared at the photo of Gia and smiled.

"Hope you like prison, baby."

It was time for the next murder, which would hopefully seal the deal.

Marshall told him what to do.

He dialed Nicoletta.

"You ready for your next performance?"

19

James couldn't sleep

This was normal when he had a murder to solve. Especially when a serial killer was on the loose. But with Gia as the main suspect? He was more motivated than ever.

He'd spent most of the night going over the details from the crime scenes, looking for similarities. Data on the ballistics and whether it was the same gun used in both shootings was still being analyzed, but it appeared that the manner of death was the same: both men had been shot dead through the forehead at close range.

So, it had to be someone they knew. Like a beautiful woman.

If he could prove that the same person killed both men, it might also clear Gia. The chances that she arrived in town and then immediately went and murdered Glass would be unlikely. Possible, but unlikely. And then to kill Rosenbloom? It didn't make any sense at all. There was zero motive.

He texted Gia even though it was two in the morning.

"Where did you go when you got to town?"

She didn't reply.

He waited a while and then texted Dante.

"Do you know what Gia did when she first got to town? Where she went?"

No response.

If he could nail this down, it might clear her name.

He printed out an enlarged picture of Gia at the crime scene and stuck it on the wall by his computer.

Although he couldn't prove it, he knew it wasn't Gia.

But so far, all the evidence, and this picture, pointed toward her.

It looked like her. If you didn't know her.

He knew that body nearly as well as he knew his own. Those thighs, tightly encased in black leather, were not the thighs he'd caressed. The shape was wrong. The ass? No way. It was not the shapely one he had fondled.

But how the fuck was that going to prove her innocence?

"Excuse me, Chief, but I know that ass and those thighs, and that is not Gia Santella."

Fucking ridiculous.

Because other than that, it could be Gia. It really could.

Sure, it could also be any other woman in the city, but it was a really tough argument when video footage at the hotel an hour earlier had shown Gia leaving the hotel in that exact get up: leather pants, black hoodie, dark sunglasses. But the camera hadn't caught her feet.

He would swear that Gia would never wear high heels with that outfit. She wore her fair share of heels but never with leather pants and a hoodie. He knew her style. He knew her taste.

But again, how was that going to prove her innocence? The chief would laugh at him.

He texted Dante again.

"Stupid question, but would Gia ever wear high heels with her leather pants and a hoodie."

To his surprise, the little bubbles on his phone appeared.

"Tacky. No."

"I didn't think so."

"If you have any more questions about Gia you are going to need to speak to our lawyer."

Damn.

"Believe it or not, I'm on your side," he wrote.

The next text he received was a shared contact for Dante's attorney.

James shook his head. Didn't Dante know he wanted to prove Gia's innocence more than anything in the world.

Even as he thought that, he had the smallest glimmer of doubt.

What if she had changed? What if something had happened to her during all the years they were apart that had turned her into a stone-cold killer without remorse? It was possible. Unlikely, but possible.

It had been a hell of a long time since they'd been together. She'd been through a lot. He suspected there had been a lot more murders on her part. After all, she'd been married to one of the most notorious drugs lords in the world.

Nico Morales had a reputation that lived long past his death.

He had killed hundreds before Gia had come into his life.

Then he supposedly stopped. Supposedly.

But who knew for sure.

James was tired and frustrated.

His phone dinged. It was Nicoletta. She sent a picture of her in a coral-colored nightie. She was in bed, leaning forward so her cleavage showed.

"Are you busy? I can't sleep. Can't you come over? I've been tossing and turning all night. I watched the *Real Housewives* entire season and am still wide awake."

He laughed. "It's three in the morning."

"I know. Please. I'll make it worth your while."

Imagining her soft body and warm bed was tempting.

"I think I could make it over."

Her place was closer to the station anyway. And there was no way he was going to sleep tonight. He'd power through. Maybe doze a little in her arms and then head to work.

"See you soon," she wrote.

20

Charles liked filming Nicoletta.

She was grace personified. She was truly the most beautiful and enticing woman he'd ever met. He felt guilty even fantasizing about Gia Santella.

Nobody could compare to Nicoletta. She was all woman—soft and feminine and so perfect for him.

They got to the roof early, and not long after they arrived, the fog lifted and the city appeared before them. The Golden Gate was lit up, and soft, white, puffy clouds seemed to float right above it.

"We are so close," Nicoletta said in a whisper.

"Yes. Hang in there, baby," he said. "Just think, in another month, we'll be on an island somewhere drinking margaritas and working on our tans."

"Can I have a pina colada instead?" she said in her baby voice.

"You can have anything you want. You can have everything you want."

She giggled.

"We're going to have a little house, and maybe…we can have a baby?"

She wrapped her arms around her belly. "Please."

"We can do whatever you want. You won't miss the opera, will you?"

"No, honey. I just want to be with you. And have a family."

There was still a slight chill in the air, so he held Nicoletta in his arms in front of him as they looked out over the rooftop.

"I love you so much," she'd said. "You are the love of my life. You are truly my soul mate."

He choked up a little. He glanced at the time. They had thirty minutes.

He kissed her neck roughly and then yanked down her leather pants. He took her right there on the roof with the entire city splayed out before them. She moaned and it turned him on so much.

She was always ready for him.

Afterward, she pulled up her pants, adjusted the black wig, and kissed him.

"You sure you can handle this, baby?" he asked, feeling suddenly protective of her. He loved her so much. He would do anything for her. He *had* done anything for her. Murder was nothing. But he didn't know if he wanted *her* to go down that dark road. "Are you 100 percent sure, baby?"

He glanced up at the surveillance camera near the door.

Marshall had hacked into hotel security and froze the camera, so it wouldn't show Nicoletta and him arriving. Five minutes before the meeting, the camera would activate again. He would hide in the shadows until after the murder. Then Nicoletta would run to the door and leave. Marshall would freeze the camera again while he snuck out and then start it up five minutes later.

His job was to just make sure he was off the roof within five minutes of the shooting. Easy peasy.

Marshall would do the rest. Instead of Nicoletta murdering Maxwell Carlton, the video footage would show Gia Santella shooting him dead in cold blood.

They'd discarded the idea of killing Jackie Fong when Oliver mentioned Carlton had gotten wind that Santella wanted to buy the hotel. He'd contacted the owner in Berlin and offered to pay double what Santella had offered.

It was the perfect motive for murder, so Charles had quickly adjusted his plans.

Nicoletta was excited about the chance to play Gia again.

"I just call his name and then walk up to him and shoot him?"

He cringed and closed his eyes. "Are you sure, baby?"

She nodded. "Yeah. I'm sure. I'll pretend it's my stepdaddy. They sort of look alike anyway."

Thinking of her stepfather and all the terrible things he had done to Nicoletta made his blood boil. Charles had killed the man after she told him. It had been his first murder. It had set the stage and laid out the path he was now on. He'd always loved Nicoletta and never regretted killing that sick son of a bitch. He'd killed him and then showered, dressed in a tuxedo, and taken Nicoletta to their senior prom. Nobody had been the wiser. They blamed it on a drug deal gone bad.

He squeezed her extra tight. "Okay, you think of Kevin, and you blow that motherfucker's head off, okay, baby?"

"I will. I got this. Don't worry," she said and patted his cheek lightly.

"I just want to make sure. You don't know what it's like to live with killing someone," he said, his voice suddenly soft. "It's not easy."

"I told you," she said. "We need to do this right. If we're going to get away with it—really get away with it forever—I have to do it. Plus, that way we're both in it, right? That way, we're bonded forever, right? Like Bonnie and Clyde?"

He winced. He wished he'd never watched that movie with her. All he wanted to say was that they both ended up dead at the end. Didn't she remember that part?

The door swung open, and she walked toward the long rectangle of light before he could stop her.

"Hi," she said in her soft baby voice.

"Nicoletta?" Carlton said, sounding confused. "I thought I was meeting..."

It was too late to stop now.

21

Fifteen minutes later...

When the phone rang, the last person I expected to hear from was on the other line.

I'd only answered the phone, hoping it was James inviting me over.

It wasn't James.

It was Maxwell Carlton, the general manager of the hotel.

"Can we meet? I have some concerns I'd like to discuss with you about the hotel and the gala. I think I know who killed Rosenbloom. But I'm afraid for my life."

I flipped on the bedside lamp and looked around as if I could find an excuse somewhere in my hotel room.

"Why me?" I asked, wondering if he knew I was a suspect.

"Because Dante trusts you," he said. "Right now, Dante is the only person I trust on that committee, and since he's not around..."

"Why don't you go to James?"

"That's another reason I want to talk to you first—to see

what you think. Then we can go to James together. You guys are old friends, right?"

"Yeah," I said and let out a sigh.

"Listen, I'm up on the restaurant roof. Can you just run up here? It will only take ten minutes. I just don't want anyone to see us talking, and during the day, there are too many people around."

Everything in me wanted to say no. But...if he knew who the killer was, it could help me clear up this nonsense with the police. I'd hear the guy out.

I was sleeping in an oversized T-shirt, so I tugged on baggy sweatpants, grabbed a thick hoodie, and stuck my feet through my furry flip-slide slippers. No reason to get too dressed up. I was just going to turn around and go straight back to bed.

The elevator dumped me in the dark restaurant, and I quickly made my way through it to the door leading to the private roof.

I pushed open the door and shivered.

It was foggy and freezing up that high.

In the distance, I heard the low bellow of a foghorn. Creepy.

Maybe this hadn't been the best idea ever. I didn't really know Carlton. He seemed nice, but what if he wanted to do something to me? If he made a move, I'd give him a swift kick in the balls. He didn't look very strong. Even if he had a weapon, I could probably take him down.

As I thought all this, I looked around. The roof appeared empty, but there was something dark by one of the huge air conditioning units. Even though the roof was lit by the hotel sign above, there were still pockets of shadow.

"Hello?"

Maybe I'd beat him there? No. He said he was already up there.

I cautiously made my way over to the dark shadows by the air conditioner.

Then I froze. It was Maxwell Carlton. He was lying on the ground.

"Mr. Carlton?"

I knelt down to feel for a pulse.

My hand came back sticky. I whipped my phone out of my pocket and turned the flashlight on. Lifeless eyes reflected in the glow.

He was dead. His head lay in a pool of blood. A pair of scissors stuck out of his neck.

I CALLED 911 first and then the hotel front desk. Then I called James.

"I got a call from the hotel's general manager, Maxwell Carlton. When I went to meet him, he was dead."

"Jesus, Gia."

"I know."

"This isn't helping your case."

"Obviously, someone is setting me up, James."

I sounded strangely calm even though I was shaking.

It didn't matter how many dead bodies I saw up close, it never didn't affect me. I had never wanted to kill people. But it had happened. I'd seen my fair share of bodies, some had died from my own hand.

"On my way. Where are you?"

"Roof above the restaurant."

"Wait? There's a dead body at your hotel?"

"The roof."

Hotel security arrived first. Two burly guys drew their weapons on me as soon as they came out the door.

"I'm the one who called."

Seeing them made me realize I'd been sitting there, unconcerned, the whole time when the killer might still have been around. Unlikely, though. I was sure Carlton had been killed as soon as we hung up and was miles away before I even made it up to the roof. It would have been stupid to stick around.

Finally, the police arrived. A red-faced young officer who looked Rose's age took me aside. Where the hell was James?

"I'm freezing," I said. My teeth were chattering, and I was shaking. "Can I at least wait in the restaurant downstairs."

He frowned and then his partner shrugged.

Down in the restaurant, I was told to sit in a corner until the detective could interview me. I wanted to drop James's name but figured they'd find out soon enough.

I was curled up in the chair and nearly asleep when a man in an overcoat and messy hair rushed in. He spoke with the police officers at the door and then they all looked over at me.

"I'm Detective Stone," he said. "I understand you are a guest at the hotel?"

"Where is the commander?" I asked and blinked.

He raised an eyebrow. "I don't know. Is there a problem?"

I reached for my phone and texted James.

"Should I talk to Detective Stone? Do I need an attorney? Where are you?"

"Something came up. Yes. Talk to Stone. Probably best if we just get this cleared up now."

I turned to the detective. "All clear to talk to you."

"I just have a few questions, then you can get back to your room. Why don't you begin with where you were right before you came up to the roof?"

I told him about the call from Maxwell Carlton.

"Do you know each other? Is it normal for him to call you in the middle of the night?"

"Not normal," I said. "I only met him the other day."

"How did he get your number?"

"Good question. I wondered the same thing," I said. "I'm assuming Dante gave it to him. But that doesn't really seem like Dante, either. Usually, he would have asked me before giving it out. Dante is my business partner. He was the one who had me join the gala fundraising committee. Which is where I met Mr. Carlton."

"Does it seem odd to you that he called?"

"Yes, very."

"But you agreed to meet him anyway?" he asked in a voice that contained no emotion but instantly felt accusatory.

I shook my head. "Yeah. In hindsight, it was sort of dumb. I guess my only excuse is that I was tired. I still have some jet lag and was in bed when he called. At the time, it seemed to make sense, but now? No."

"And he said he was calling because he had information about Rosenbloom's death?"

"That's what he said."

"But you just met?"

I nodded. "Listen," I said. "It doesn't make any sense to me either."

A woman in a beige trench coat and shaggy hair called his name. When I looked over, her eyes were cold.

"Excuse me," he said and got up. "My partner is calling me."

As soon as he walked away, I texted James.

"What the fuck is going on? Why aren't you here. I'm starting to think my attorney should be here and I shouldn't be saying shit."

He didn't respond for a few seconds. While I waited, I watched the detective and his partner across the room. They were speaking and glancing my way every once in a while.

My phone buzzed.

"Chief thinks I'm too close to the case. Called me off."

"Motherfuck." I typed.

The female detective opened her phone and looked at something. Then the detective nodded and came back.

"You and your partner are planning to buy this hotel, I hear?"

I clamped my mouth shut. How did he know. How did they find out so quickly?

I glanced over at the detective. She was speaking to the hotel manager, who had just arrived.

"We were trying to keep it on the down-low," I said. "I was doing some investigation into financial inconsistencies before the sale went through, so we could find out who might be embezzling."

The detective cocked his head. "Is this something you've done in the past?"

I shook my head. "Not really."

"Huh."

He looked down at this notebook. I glanced over. It was a bunch of indecipherable scribbles.

I yawned. "Are we done? I think if you have any more questions I should have you speak to my attorney." *Despite what James thinks.*

"One more question. Were you aware that Maxwell Carlton had also made a bid to buy the hotel?"

"What?" I was genuinely surprised. I shook my head. "No. I just got into town the other day from out of the country. Dante has been handling all of this for me. We were supposed to meet about the particulars next week."

"Apparently, Mr. Carlton offered one million more than the asking price yesterday."

How the fuck does he know all of this? I was confused.

"Yesterday?"

"We were only aware of it because he called our office this morning, saying that he had received a threatening phone call telling him to withdraw his offer or he'd be sorry."

"You're fucking kidding me?" I blurted. What the fuck was going on?

I could feel my face grow warm. This was insane.

The detective looked at me, working his mouth in a weird way. He was chewing on the inside of his lip as he watched me.

"Do you think that's why he wanted to meet with me?"

I realized that this man was not on my side. He was looking at me as a suspect. It was time for me to bail.

"I'm done here. If you need to speak to me again, you can contact my attorney."

He nodded. "We'll be in touch."

I didn't answer. I felt his partner's eyes on me as I walked toward the elevator. I didn't like the way she was looking at me. I didn't like the direction the detective's questions had gone. It had been a huge mistake to talk to them both without an attorney. But James had told me it was okay to talk to Stone. And James was on my side. Or was he?

22

I waited until morning to call Dante, but wasn't able to sleep at all.

Something was fucked up, and I seemed to have landed right in the middle of it all.

When dawn broke, I dialed Dante's number.

He was not an early riser. The restaurant business was a late-night game.

"Everything okay?" were his first words.

"I'm not sure."

I told him everything.

"This isn't good, Gia," he said. "I can't believe James had you speak to the detectives without an attorney."

"Yeah. Now I realize it was a mistake. A big one."

"What was he thinking?"

"Did you know he made a bid? Carlton?"

"No. It's odd. It doesn't make sense. I talked to him about the possibility of making an offer, and he told me I'd be making a mistake," Dante said. "At the time, I thought it was because he thought it was a losing proposition. Maybe I misunderstood. I had no idea he wanted to buy the hotel. I had no idea he had the money to do so until just recently, when we started looking into the embezzlement."

"How does he?"

"Not quite sure yet. It sure makes him a suspect in the embezzling situation, right?"

"A dead suspect."

"Oh boy," Dante said.

"I don't like the way the cops are talking to me, Dante. They are trying to establish a motive."

"They can try whatever they want. They can't pin a murder on you that you didn't commit."

I frowned. "I'm not so sure."

"I'm coming up there," he said. "won't be in until late tonight. I have some things to take care of down here first. I'll book a room there, and let's meet for breakfast?"

I instantly felt relief. "Thank you."

"Don't worry. Your attorney is top notch. I wouldn't hire anyone else."

"I know."

After I hung up, I was filled with relief and exhaustion at the same time. My all-nighter finally hit me. Knowing Dante was coming took all the fight out of me. I could relax. I rummaged around until I found an old melatonin tablet and, after popping that, crawled into bed.

I slept until two in the afternoon.

When I woke, my phone showed several messages. And the hotel phone was blinking. I played the voice message back on it first. It was Detective Stone.

"We'd like you to come down to the station this afternoon, at your convenience, for some follow up questions."

I hit delete.

While I was listening to the messages, James texted. "We still on for dinner? Five at my place?"

Um, yeah. He had some explaining to do.

"Sure. Unless I'm in jail for murder. What the fuck James? I'm supposed to come down to the station now. Why did you let me talk to them without an attorney?"

I held my breath, watching the text bubbles until his message popped up: "You're going to have to trust me. I'm working on it."

That wasn't very reassuring.

I dialed Dante. He didn't answer. He was probably on the plane already. I sent a text message. "Detectives want me to come down to station. Help."

After I sent it, I worried it made me look guilty. *Fuck.* I already felt guilty even though I hadn't done a damn thing but haul my ass out of bed to go talk to some stranger.

Who ended up murdered before I arrived.

Fuck. Fuck. Fuck.

I took a long, hot shower and tried to forget about the detective's message. I replayed the words he used in my mind and analyzed each one.

Saying, "At your convenience," made it seem like it wasn't a big deal. But maybe that was his ploy.

After my shower, I stood in front of the windows, naked. There were no other adjacent buildings as tall as this one, which meant I wouldn't be staring at anyone across the way. What this hotel—this suite—needed more than anything were the decks I was planning on adding to every single suite. Having the ability to step outside of your hotel room made all the difference in the world.

I was itching for fresh air.

I dressed in some faded, black jeans and an even more faded black T-shirt, slipped on my converse sneakers, and headed downstairs.

I wore my dark sunglasses and stuck my ear pods in my ears,

even though I wasn't listening to anything. It was my shield against unwanted personal interaction. It always worked. Most of the time, I did it to thwart unwelcome advances from men on airplanes or public transportation, but today I just didn't want to engage with anyone at all.

No offense to the nice older woman with the dog who stepped into the elevator on the seventh floor. I gave her a small smile and then stared straight ahead.

Downstairs, I ordered an espresso and bacon and gruyere egg bites at the café and then headed outside to sit.

The fog had lifted and there was a small square of sunshine at one of the outside café tables. I plopped down and thought about the murder.

This was the third person on the board that had been murdered.

It was crazy that someone was out there killing people because they objected to the *Death of Engleberg*. But the fact was, death threats *had* been received.

And there were no limits to crazy in this world.

I'd done a little research after the first meeting and saw that Engleberg's daughters had pleaded for peace when there had been protests at the Chicago opening.

So...*they* were out as suspects.

But who would care enough to murder people to make their point?

What was the motive?

Speaking of, if the detectives suspected me, there *was* motive. Which sucked.

My cell rang. Unknown caller.

"Santella."

"This is Detective Stone."

I didn't answer. I let him fill the awkward silence.

"Do you have a few minutes? I have a few more questions for you. I'm at your hotel."

I swiveled my head. He was standing on the sidewalk in front of the lobby doors. He looked around and then our eyes met and held. *Fuck me.*

He gave a half-hearted wave. "Can I crash your lunch?"

"It's breakfast," I said and hung up.

He pulled out a chair at my table before I could put my sunglasses back on. Luckily, the sun had shifted, lighting up my face, so I had a good excuse. For some reason, I didn't want to meet his probing gaze.

"You know," he said. "I've got a couple discrepancies in the timeline and details of last night."

I ignored him and sipped my coffee. It burned my tongue, but I pretended it was fine. I'd let him talk. I'd find out what he had on me. He could talk. I'd stay silent.

"We checked Maxwell Carlton's phone, and it didn't show any calls to you. In fact, it didn't show any outgoing calls at all last night."

"*What?*" I spit the word out along with a little coffee. I'd vowed not to say a word but it had slipped out.

He shook his head. "There's no record of him calling you."

I narrowed my eyes. That didn't make sense.

"We checked with his wife, and she said he received a call and left unexpectedly without any explanation."

He paused, waiting for my answer.

I wasn't going to say jack shit.

Just then a big black car pulled up, and Dante hopped out.

He must've taken an earlier flight. *Thank God.*

I stood. "Dante!"

He turned and saw me. His face lit up in a huge grin. But then he saw the detective at my table, and his smile disappeared.

He was beside us in a few seconds.

The detective stood and introduced himself. Dante said he was my business partner.

Before the detective sat back down, Dante cleared his throat.

"Detective, I appreciate your diligence in solving this horrific crime. As an acquaintance of Mr. Carlton, I'm devastated by his death. And as potential future owners of this hotel, the last thing Ms. Santella and I would ever want is for a murder to be associated with our hotel. I'm a practical businessman and, without sounding cold-hearted, this isn't great for business. I'm sure you understand," he said coolly. "So, the sooner this is solved, the sooner we can move on and put it past us. With that said, how can I help? If you have any more questions for Ms. Santella, I'd like them asked with her attorney present."

Detective Stone seemed a bit unnerved.

I liked Dante's play—obviously, as future owners, the last thing we wanted was a murder at our hotel. So, duh, I couldn't possibly be a suspect.

But the detective didn't bite.

"We have a few discrepancies I'm trying to clear up with your business partner. As I'm sure you're aware, she was the one who found Mr. Carlton's body."

Dante raised an eyebrow. "Yes?"

"According to Ms. Santella, Mr. Carlton called and asked her to meet him. But we show no record on his phone of the call. Even though he said he was already on the roof, and we did find his cell phone on his body," he paused, but didn't leave room for a response. "In addition, Mr. Carlton's wife said that he received a call at their home earlier that night and left as if he had been summoned to a meeting."

Dante nodded but only said, "How can we help you?"

The detective stared for a minute and then stood.

"I'll let you know." He slid his card toward Dante and then another one toward me.

We watched him walk away and waited until the valet had brought his car before we spoke.

"Motherfuck," I said.

"He's hot for you."

I sighed. "And not the kind of hot I want."

Dante shook his head. "Definitely not that kind."

The way he said it made me look at him. "He's gay?"

"Oh yeah."

"Not that it matters," we both said at the same time and laughed. It was a weak laugh, but still a laugh. And it felt good. I hadn't realized how stressed out I was.

We stood.

"I'm going to check in to my room and then make some calls," Dante said. "Want to meet for dinner."

Instantly, I felt guilty even though I knew I shouldn't.

"What?" he said, picking up on it.

"I'm having dinner with James."

"Don't say squat about the murders," he said. "I know he's on your side, but just to be safe."

"I won't. The last thing I want to do is talk about that."

He laughed. "I bet I know what you want to talk about. Or *not* talk about I should say."

I ignored his innuendo.

"Breakfast?"

"Knowing you two, let's make it lunch."

"Stop!"

I instantly felt better. Dante would fix everything.

23

Despite Tony's generous offer to drive me around, I didn't want to disturb his "grandpa time," so I'd arranged for the long-term rental of a Bugatti. It was also a test run of how rentals would work for my hotel guests one day. I would probably try out a few of the luxury car rental places in the city to see who was best.

So far, this one wasn't bad. The car was dropped off in front of the hotel. When I got down there, the valet was waiting for me. As soon as I got behind the wheel and pulled out of the hotel driveway, I knew it was the right call. I'd missed driving high-performance vehicles. For so many years living in Barcelona, I hadn't needed a car.

But I loved the feel of a powerful engine purring. I made a note to myself to make a trip down to the Laguna Seca raceway and take a few spins around the track. It was where I'd learned to drive as well as any race car driver—or cop in pursuit. The skill had served me well over the years. Yes, I'd take it to the racetrack and stop by Monterey to visit my parent's graves. I would also take it to drive to Darling's house in the next week or so.

Right now, it would get me to see James.

I pulled my car up to the address James had given me and peeked out my window at the building before me.

It was an apartment in the Sunset district.

There was not a parking spot for miles around. I'd started looking as soon as I pulled onto his street. But as I sat there, the garage door rolled open, and I saw James sitting there with a grin. He gestured for me to pull in.

I rolled down the window as I got beside him. "Hey, sailor."

"Park in spot twenty-three."

"See you in a sec."

He was waiting by an elevator in one corner.

I walked over and leaned down to kiss his cheek. He turned his head and our lips met.

I didn't pull back. I felt his arms reach for me and pull me down. His hands were in my hair, and in the darkness of the garage, we made out like teenagers.

When I finally had the willpower to pull back, he gave me a naughty grin.

"Oh, James, you are trouble."

"Look who's talking."

"Am I really a suspect?"

He frowned. "I'm working on it. It makes no sense. I'll figure it out. Let's just forget about it for a few hours and catch up on the past ten years."

"Sounds good," I said and instantly felt better. If James wasn't worried about it, I wasn't. He pushed the button to summon the elevator. Then he tugged on my hand and pulled me down, kissing me again.

We both jumped when the elevator dinged and the door slid open.

"Jesus. I thought I'd have more willpower," he said as he

wheeled his chair into the elevator. "I'm sorry, Gia. We can't do this."

"I know," I said. "We can't."

"Have to stop," he said.

"Absolutely."

I was flustered and ready to rip off his clothes.

"I'm serious, Gia. I'm seeing someone."

"Does Madame Butterfly know we're having dinner."

The elevator doors whooshed open onto his floor.

"She trusts me. She knows we used to date," he said.

"Used to date? Talk about reducing us to nothing."

"I didn't mean that."

"You told her? About us?"

"You know me, Gia. I'm brutally honest and upfront about everything."

"To a fault."

"Hey, hey, now," he said, spinning the wheels on his wheelchair to maneuver himself in front of his door. "We don't need to start that."

"Am I wrong?"

"Damn, you are as spicy as ever. I thought age would've mellowed you."

"Hardly."

He laughed. "So, good to see you, darling."

My heart melted right then. Calling me darling instantly turned me to mush.

A few seconds later, he opened the door to his condo, and I followed him into a well-lit space with steel and black leather furnishings. Uber masculine. Like James.

A table was already set. Something was simmering on the stove and the apartment smelled divine.

"I don't remember you being a gourmet chef, but I think even Dante would be jealous at how this place smells," I said.

He was already at the stove. I noticed that all his counters were lowered so he could work with ease. He was stirring this and flipping that.

"Can I help?"

He looked over his shoulder. "Yes, pour us some of that red."

I grabbed the bottle. "Yummy. You don't have to tell me twice."

Before I took a sip, I brought a glass over to James and set it on the counter.

"That looks amazing."

"Get!" he said and shooed me away.

"Fine." I said in a huffy voice and then walked around his place, checking it out. "Where's your bathroom."

He told me. I peeked into the bedrooms as I passed. Both sterile with few personal touches. Much like the rest of his place.

When I came out, the table was set with dishes of food.

"Sit," he said. "I'll be right back."

He headed down the hall. On my way to the table, I paused at a small table. It had a picture of him with his wife and daughter.

I picked it up.

I stared at it, my heart breaking for James. I looked around the rest of the room. That photo was the only indication that she'd ever existed. I shook my head.

That's when I noticed it was quiet. I turned and James was behind me.

He gave me a smile.

"She was the love of my life, Gia."

"I know," I said solemnly.

"You hungry?" he said in a chipper voice as I followed him to the table.

"Starved." *In more ways than one.*

"Dig in."

After we ate steak with a parsley-flaked butter sauce and creamy garlic mashed potatoes and delicate asparagus, I sat back, moaning with pleasure.

"Good God that was good."

"I was not messing around."

"I guess not."

"Let's go out on the deck with our wine," he said.

I followed him out. The view on his small deck was of the street below. But I didn't care about a view.

I sat in an Adirondack chair, and James sat beside me. There was a salty breeze coming in from the Pacific and, as the sun dipped lower on the horizon, I felt a chill run through me.

James, ever attentive, noticed.

"You okay?"

"I can't believe I'm a murder suspect."

"Gia, I can't talk about it."

I turned to him in surprise. "You're kidding, right?"

He sighed loudly. "If you want my help. If you want me to work to prove you didn't do it, we can't discuss it. I promised the chief."

"Of course you did."

One thing about James. He'd uphold the letter of the law even if it meant he was going to prison for life. That had been, and always would be, the thing that kept us apart. I didn't see things as black and white as he did.

"I'm not going to change you now," I said, lightly. "Just make sure you prove my innocence. This is starting to become a pain in the ass."

He seemed relieved I let it go.

"Let's go in. I'll turn on the fire," he said.

Inside, the flames on the gas stove leaped to life, shooting warmth out into the room. James went around dimming lights and lighting candles. "Go pick some music out," he said over his shoulder.

He had two crates full of vinyl records next to a turntable. I wanted something sultry, moody. I put on "Waiting Game" by Banks. He crooked a finger at me slowly with a sensual grin.

I caught my breath. His eyes locked on mine. We both knew it was a foregone conclusion what would happen next.

But I was nervous. It had been a long time.

And I didn't want to fall for him again. That was dangerous. And could only end badly.

24

I was on his lap when the doorbell rang.

What the fuck?

I jumped up and pulled my top back up over my naked breasts.

James looked guiltily down at the tent in his pants and quickly pulled a pillow onto his lap.

I was sitting on a barstool, sipping wine when he opened the door.

Nicoletta was standing there.

Her pink lips opened into a big O.

"Shoot," she said. "I forgot tonight was your dinner—catching up on old times."

She started to back up.

James reached for her hand.

"Come on in. It's fine."

I hid my anger. It was not fucking fine.

I hopped up and grabbed my bag.

"I was just leaving," I said. I leaned down and gave James a kiss on the cheek. "Thanks for dinner, sailor."

Then I was gone.

I tried not to peel out of the garage, knowing that bitch was upstairs feeling smug as fuck.

Furious, I drove around not wanting to go back to my hotel room.

I'd honestly thought that I would be staying all night with James. I had made up this scenario in my head where we woke together and made love and then I would make him breakfast...

I cringed thinking of this.

I'd made up this romantic scenario in my head. And why?

I hated to admit it, but I was lonely.

So fucking lonely.

And I'd looked to James, subconsciously, to fill that void.

It wasn't fair to him. It wasn't fair to me.

Frustrated, sad, and forlorn, I did what I always did when I felt this way—I headed to the closest bar. I valet parked and scooted up to the crowded bar. The bartender was busy at the other end. A guy to my right with a big bushy beard said, "I got this" after I'd attempted and failed to order two different times.

"Yo, Connie!" he said with a New York accent.

The waitress, a skinny woman with flushed cheeks and thin hair scraped back in a ponytail was in front of us.

"I'll take another lager and whatever this one wants."

I ordered a tequila, and when it arrived I toasted the bearded guy. "Thank you."

"No problem. You looked like you needed that."

"Amen, brother," I said. I wondered if my mascara was smeared. I'm not going to lie, a few tears slipped out when I was driving away from James's apartment.

"My name is Red," he said.

"I'm Gia. Next one's on me Red."

My phone pinged. I looked down. It was a text from James.

"Call me."

I ignored it. I wasn't ready to analyze our fucked-up relationship any more. I was done. I needed a break from the emotional roller coaster. At least for the night.

For starters, I knew James. He was beating himself up for making out with me even though he had a girlfriend. His guilt was annoying. I didn't want to deal with it. So I wasn't going to.

I bought Red a few drinks. He bought me a few. He was from New Jersey, in the city on business and had five kids at home. We talked baseball and, ultimately, Spain.

His wife was from a small town in southern Spain.

At the end of the night, I got up to leave, and he grabbed my elbow when I lost my balance.

"Hey, Gia, don't take this the wrong way, but I'm going to call you a ride, okay?"

I nodded my thanks.

I nearly fell asleep in the car on the way back to the hotel. I pulled my sunglasses on when I got there so I didn't have to make eye contact with the valets or the people in the front lobby as I made my way to the elevator.

Once in my room, I flopped on the bed. My phone buzzed again and I ignored it. James had called and texted a few times while I was at the bar.

I'd deal with him again in the morning.

When I woke, it was a typical San Francisco late morning— gray and cold. I saw that James had not stopped calling and that Dante had joined in with four of his own calls.

Fuck.

I would have to deal with them soon.

Meanwhile, I sheepishly called Tony and asked if he and a friend could get the Bugatti back to my hotel from the bar where I'd parked it the night before.

I put on the coffee and then unpeeled my dress and stepped into the hot shower.

Only after a cup of coffee in me did I dial James.

"Yo."

"Gia, where the fuck have you been?"

"What's up?" I said nonchalantly.

"There's some pretty strong evidence that points to you. I'm not sure there is anything I can do to help you."

"Whatever. Dante is handling it." I said. "Did Madame Butterfly say you couldn't help prove my innocence because we nearly fucked last night?"

I was pissed.

He gave a loud sigh. "That evidence, Gia, it's bad. You need to be perfectly honest with me. I shouldn't even be talking to you."

"What is it now, James? Another shitty photograph?"

"Video. Hotel surveillance footage. It shows you shooting Maxwell Carlton."

"That's impossible."

25

I needed help.

A video of me? That was some high-tech shit, since I obviously did not kill anyone and yet there was a video showing me murdering someone.

I hung up with James and called Danny. I already felt guilty that I'd been in town so long without letting him know. But how did I know things were going to hell so quickly and that I'd become a murder suspect?

Danny always been a night owl, so I knew when I called that he was either still up or had just gone to bed with the sunrise.

As a millennial who didn't speak on the phone, I could hear the surprise in his voice when he answered. "Gia?"

"Long story short. I'm in the city. There's a video of me shooting someone dead. I need your help."

I heard some shuffling sounds. "At your service."

Then: "You're in San Francisco?"

"I was going to surprise you."

"Um, you did."

"Can I come over."

"I'll make coffee."

"What? So sophisticated."

"Haha, Gia."

I disconnected.

I dressed in a faded pair of black jeans, my heeled motorcycle boots, a soft T-shirt and my black Armani blazer.

As soon as the wheels of the Bugatti hit the pavement of the Tenderloin district, my heart sunk. My once-beloved working neighborhood was gentrified. Boutique coffee shops. High-end restaurants. Shiny silver skyscraper apartment buildings.

I could hardly believe it.

And still, tent cities on the sidewalks housed the homeless.

Meanwhile, young men with slouchy stocking caps, goatees, and flannel shirts with Armani sneakers were walking the streets. Women dressed in Lululemon leggings, carrying lattes and pushing their dogs in tiny strollers gathered on corners, wearing their Tiffany sunglasses on top of their balayage-blonde heads.

It was fucking bizarre.

I hated it.

My neighborhood was now home to a bunch of hipsters.

My brief idea to buy another apartment in the TL was immediately discarded.

This neighborhood was no longer my kind of scene.

As I looked for a parking spot outside my building, I decided to pull into the spot near the homeless guy the mommy crowd had just dismissed.

He didn't look over when my alarm beeped loudly as I set it.

"Hey," I said.

He kept walking. I jogged to reach his side. "What's your name?"

"Roland," he mumbled and kept walking.

"Hey," I said again, keeping pace with him as he walked. He side-eyed me.

"You busy, Roland?" I asked.

He stopped and laughed. I laughed too. His teeth weren't bad for a homeless guy. And his face was freshly shaven.

"No, seriously. I need your help."

He drew back and gave me a skeptical look.

"I'll pay you to watch my car," I said and jerked my chin back toward the Bugatti.

He looked and blinked. "Yeah?"

"Yeah. Twenty bucks to start screaming if anyone gets near it? I'm just going to be right there." I pointed toward the building.

He shrugged. I pulled out a ten. "I'll give you the other ten when I come back in about an hour."

He nodded and headed back toward the car. I watched him slouch against the wall near the car before I rang the doorbell.

The camera swiveled to point at me. I held up my middle finger.

The door clicked open. Inside, the lobby looked great. I'd told Danny to do whatever he wanted with the building, and I'd pay for it all. He'd installed beautiful paintings of different San Francisco scenes. I loved it. I raced up the stairs. He was waiting at the top of the landing with his arms wide. I was enveloped in his hug. He smelled like woodsy spices.

My heart filled with gratitude. I'd never expected him to live this long. He had a disease that made him grow too much and too fast, but some new experimental drug treatment had arrested his growth and prolonged his life indefinitely.

"What are you doing here?" he asked.

I stepped inside my old loft.

In the old days, Danny had lived in a tiny, cramped apartment a few blocks away that was full of computer monitors and old pizza boxes.

One corner of the loft still held all the monitors he needed to be the world-class hacker he was, but he'd closed it off into a dark room. I could see the bank of computers flickering green lights from the door to the room that was ajar.

I nodded that way. "That was smart."

"Yeah, that equipment doesn't do well in the light."

The other area was a very tasteful masculine apartment with dark wood and muted tones. And it was neat as a pin.

"Looks good, Danny."

He blushed.

Steam was starting to bloom out of a kettle on the stove.

"I'm making a pour-over. You want some?"

"You're so fancy," I said, teasing.

He blushed again.

"Can we drink it on the roof?" I asked.

"Sure." The roof was always my favorite part of my loft apartment.

With steaming mugs of coffee—that I had to admit was delicious—we headed up the stairs to the roof.

My old pergola covered in grape vines was doing well. It even looked like it had a fresh coat of paint. We sat on the upholstered furniture.

"It's so great to see you."

"I'm back for good, I think," I said.

For a second he froze and said, "I can move out tomorrow."

"No fucking way," I said. "I'm buying a hotel. I'm going to live there."

"What?" he spluttered, nearly spitting out his coffee.

I think I was nearly as shocked as he was. I'd never intended to live in my hotel. But seeing the Tenderloin and realizing it was no longer my home, made it feel like the right decision.

"I was wondering if you wanted to buy this place?" I said nonchalantly.

He frowned. "The loft?"

"No, the whole building."

A flush instantly spread from his neck up to his cheeks.

He looked down. "Gia, I don't think I can afford it. I mean that's a super generous offer."

I reached over and opened a small box stashed under a planter. Danny looked at me wide-eyed. I winked as I opened it. It had a metal cigarette case and lighter. I lit one and blew out the smoke before I answered.

"Not bad for a cigarette that's probably a decade old," I said. I ashed the cigarette and then smiled at Danny. "Here's the thing. Way I figure it, with the rent-to-own plan we've had in place, you've already put a substantial down payment on it. Your mortgage wouldn't be too crazy. In fact, your mortgage would be exactly what you pay for rent right now."

I waited for his reaction.

He shook his head and exhaled. "That's great, but nobody is going to give me a loan. I'm an off-the-grid hacker," he said ruefully.

"Oh, yeah," I said, inhaling the stale smoke again. "I forgot to tell you. I'm the bank. It's contract for deed. Just keep doing exactly what you're doing, and you'll own the building and have the title. The rent you collect from your tenants will easily pay the property taxes."

"Gia, I can't."

"You can," I said.

He shook his head again.

"But that's not why I'm here."

"Deepfake," he said.

"Huh?"

"The video of you. Someone who knows Deepfake technology."

"Is that the Tom Cruise TikTok thing?"

"Yeah, that was the most famous one. And the hologram of

Kim Kardashian's dead father. And the video of Joaquin Oliver asking people to vote."

I hadn't heard of any of these those videos. I also had no idea who the last name was.

"Joaquin Oliver?"

Danny told me Joaquin Oliver was a high school student killed in the Parkland shooting. His parents had a Deepfake video made of him telling people to vote for gun safety.

"Creepy," I said.

"Nah. Effective."

"What did they make Obama do?"

"There's ones of Trump, too," he said. "And Daisy Ridley having sex. And Adolf Hitler. Obviously, all fake. Oh, not to mention those ads that ran with Russian president Vladimir Putin and North Korean leader Kim Jong-un."

"Holy shit," I said. "I've missed a lot. All I know is this all sounds dangerous as fuck."

"It is," Danny said sounding distracted. "From what I understand Deepfake relies on what's called an auto encoder, an artificial neural network—"

"English, please," I interrupted.

"Okay, it's like this—This network compresses and encodes data, say from a video, and then reconstructs it. So basically, it's breaking down images and videos of you and then superimposing them on a model who is representing you," he said.

"I still don't really get it."

"That's okay," he said.

"How do we prove it's not me?"

"I'm not sure. It's damn good technology."

"Apparently," I said. "It was enough to make James believe it."

"Oh shit."

"I know."

"It might take a while, but I'll research what people do to show it's fake."

"Thanks." I stood. "Listen I have to go. I'll send over the paperwork tomorrow for the building purchase."

In my eyes, it was a fair deal. I didn't want the building anymore. I didn't need the money. Danny had helped me out for free for more years than I could count by managing the building and hacking into any computer system in the world that I asked him to. He deserved to be financially secure. Not to mention, he'd risked his life before to help me. It was totally a fair deal.

"Gia!" he started to protest, but I was already down the stairs and out the door.

"I'll have Dante send you that video," I said over my shoulder.

Danny was good people.

I slipped the homeless guy a twenty-dollar bill and roared off in the Bugatti, shaking my head at my old neighborhood with its juice bars, barre studios, and boutique baby shops. I wouldn't miss it at all.

My phone rang as soon as I got in the car.

"Gia, about the building..."

"Prove that video isn't me," I said and hung up before he could say anything else.

26

Back at the hotel, I was just ordering a smoothie from room service when Dante called.

"I just spoke to your lawyer and James."

"You spoke to James?" I interrupted.

He continued. "And we all agreed you should leave town for a few days."

"What?"

"If you're not in town and more people end up dead you'll have an alibi."

That was crazy, but I couldn't argue with the logic.

"I'll go see Darling."

Darling had moved to Mill Valley in Marin.

"Great," Dante said. "Stay put until you hear from me."

I didn't answer.

Within an hour, I was driving across the Golden Gate bridge. Seagulls swooped above me, and the sun was out. Life wasn't so bad.

In fact, it would be pretty damn good if I could only figure out who was killing people and why they were framing me for it.

I hadn't even been in town long enough to be the target for a framing. Had I? Odd as fuck.

It had to be someone on the gala foundation committee. That narrowed it down to thirteen people? Or less.

As I drove, a man in a Lamborghini pulled up beside me. I only noticed because he was matching my speed, staying abreast of me, and it was annoying. When I looked over, he gave a slight nod and revved his engine. Then he lifted his polarized sunglasses and gave me a slow wink. I slammed on the brakes so he flew ahead of me. Oh brother.

Then, in response, he punched his brakes, and I went roaring past. I laughed when I saw his face. He saluted me and then I left him in the dust, watching his vehicle get smaller in my rearview mirror.

The rest of the drive was uneventful, and soon I was pulling into Darling's circular drive.

My city friend lived in an old-fashioned classic Tudor with steep, gabled peaks and roof and banks of windows above a brick foundation. It was tucked into a deep forested area and fronted by a massive green lawn. It was lovely.

As soon as I came to a stop, the door was flung open and a pack of golden retrievers raced out toward my car.

I leaped out and laughed, smothered by wiggling, furry bodies so I didn't get a chance to see Darling until she let out a sharp whistle.

She stood in the entry and looked as awesome as ever.

Darling was like a lioness, a queen—a powerful, strong, beautiful member of the royal family of humanity. She had massive, golden cat eyes, lined thickly with kohl like an Egyptian goddess and those ridiculously long, black eyelashes.

Her Rubenesque body was encased in a peach silk jumpsuit. She wore high-heeled sandals, and her black hair fell down her back in elaborate braids.

"Gia-Fucking-Santella," she said with a naughty grin and held out her arms.

I raced over and hugged her.

"I swear, woman, you don't age," I said as I pulled back.

"Same, girl. Same."

A woman dressed in beige slacks, high heels, and a coral silk blouse appeared behind Darling.

"This is Cora," Darling said. "She keeps me sane."

"Pleasure to meet you," the woman said. She had brown hair pulled back tightly in a bun and a no-nonsense attitude. "Your first meeting begins in one hour."

"I know, I know," Darling said and fluttered one hand with long, gold-painted nails. "Gia, I couldn't get out of some meetings this morning. I'm going to set you up by the pool with some margaritas and my favorite gals from the nail salon. They're going to give you a mani-pedi while I'm doing business."

I laughed. "Not necessary. I can amuse myself for a few hours."

"Mmmhhhmm," she said and winked. "Keep your hands off my pool boy."

"No promises."

We both burst into laughter.

"Your juice is ready." Cora said and then consulted her clipboard. "You have fifty-five minutes now."

"Come on in," Darling said. "I've got to drink my green juice before I forget. Want one?"

"Nope."

In the kitchen, Darling told me she'd become an angel investor.

Hard-luck cases—all run by women—sought her funding.

While she had a soft heart for anyone who was struggling, Darling was also a sharp businesswoman and wouldn't invest in anything she didn't think had a shot.

For those who didn't have a clue and approached her for help, she almost always pointed them to other resources to help them get to where they needed to be.

She told me about a young woman she'd talked to the previous week who had run away to escape her alcoholic parents and was working as a waitress. She had several good business ideas but didn't have the wherewithal to follow through. Seeing her potential, Darling wrote her a check to pay for a college education.

"You start there," she'd told the woman. "When you have your degree, come back and let's talk again."

Six hours later, armed with new blood-red fingernails and toenails and a bronze body from lying by the pool all day, I got back into my car.

Despite Dante's orders, I didn't feel like staying over. I was restless. I wanted to get back to the city and try to find who was setting me up. I wasn't going to be able to do that from Marin County. If James and Dante and my attorney wanted me out of town, I was coming back. I wasn't doing a damn bit of good here at Darling's house.

"You sure you don't want to stay, baby."

Darling had changed into a flowy African-style dress that she wore with four-inch high slides.

"I'm good. Let's talk soon," I said. "It's been amazing to see you."

"Mmmhhhmm. Like we never were apart."

I hugged her and was enveloped by her soft warmth.

She wasn't that much older than me, and was more like a sister than a mother, but something about her made me feel safe like when my mama hugged me as a little girl.

I watched her in my rearview mirror as she waved goodbye.

About halfway back to San Francisco my phone dinged.

The car played back the message for me over the speakers. It was from Dante.

"They're going to issue an arrest warrant."

27

I pulled over to the gravel shoulder. The road was steep and windy behind me, and anyone coming around the sharp curve a little too loosely might rear-end me because the shoulder wasn't very wide. I decided I wouldn't park there for long.

"They can't do that."

"Oh, they can," Dante said. "It sounds like you're driving. Where are you? You were supposed to stay with Darling." His annoyance was plain in his voice.

"I never do what I'm supposed to, Dante. You should know that about me by now," I said. "Run this by me again, and make it quick, I'm perched on the edge of a cliff on Witch Mountain."

I squinted into the rearview mirror. A huge black Ram truck came around the corner. My heart raced, but the driver must've seen me and quickly moved into the opposite lane.

Right behind him, a little sports car came zipping around the corner, but this driver was hugging the curve at the white line, giving me plenty of room.

"Huh? Witch Mountain?" Dante said.

"James called me, and he was super sketchy sounding,"

Dante said. "He wanted to know where you were. I didn't tell him."

I paused. *Fuck.*

"Don't come back. Not until I speak to your attorney and figure out what he wants us to do."

"Bye," I said and hung up.

I cranked the stereo for the rest of my drive back to the city.

Before she disappeared, Rose had gotten me hooked on hip hop, which was something that I hadn't paid much attention to in the past. I knew it was slightly ridiculous for a woman my age to be singing along at the top of her lungs to Kanye West's song "Monster," but something about Nicki Minaj's badass rapping and animalistic growls in the song sent chills through me. She was magnetic. Listening to loud music made the drive back go quickly.

By the time I got back to my hotel room, I was ready to fall into bed and sleep for ten hours. I was ignoring the fact that the police wanted to arrest me for murder. I just couldn't deal with it right then. I'd get a good night sleep and figure out what to do in the morning. They weren't ready to arrest me yet. At least I hoped not.

The next morning, I woke to brilliant sunlight streaming in through the skylight above the bed. I yawned and did some stretches and then some sit-ups and pushups.

They hurt. I was incredibly out of shape.

But that would change. I decided that, rather than sit around and wait for the cops to arrest me, I was going to go about my normal life until the attorney told me not to. That meant to continue the plans I'd already made.

Part of my plans involved catching up with all my old friends. This morning, I was visiting my good friend and sensei Kato. He would kick my ass back into shape quickly.

Besides, I needed a distraction from worrying about a

possible murder rap. After my workout, I'd go visit Danny again. See if he had any luck with the Deepfake video of me.

I couldn't wait to see Kato.

Many years before, when I was just a kid who had moved to the big city and was drowning my grief over my parent's death with booze, sex, and other unsavory behavior, Budo Karate via Kato, had saved my life.

I tugged on some leggings, a hoodie, and my sneakers and ate some hard-boiled eggs I'd ordered from room service. I left the hotel incognito, with dark sunglasses and my hoodie pulled up over my head, and ran to Chinatown, arriving sweaty and breathless at the door to the Dojo.

I leaned down, putting my palms on my knees to catch my breath before I rang the doorbell.

"Looks like we've got a lot of work to do."

The familiar voice brought a smile to my face.

Standing up, I saw Kato there before me, holding the keys to the Dojo.

He still wore his sleek, black hair longer in the back, and his toned and fit body would still put Michelangelo's David to shame

I squealed and grabbed him in a bear hug. He was a little stiff, but that was his nature.

"Gia San, it's been a long time, my friend," he said.

"Kato! I can't fucking believe it. You haven't aged a day, you bastard."

"Nice to see you too," he said and chuckled as he unlocked the door. "When did you get back to the States?"

"Just the other day," I said, grinning. "How's Susie and the kids?"

He shook his head. "Susie is the same. My princess. The kids? Oh boy. Teenagers are hell on earth."

"That's a fact," I said, following up the stairs to the main room of the Dojo.

"Let's get right to work," he said as we entered the room and he dumped a water bottle and duffel bag on a small table. "My first class is in an hour. We can catch up over lunch or something soon."

I smiled. I didn't tell him I was a murder suspect and could end up in jail any second. Still in denial, I guess.

We spent the next hour working out and catching up during pauses. His youngest son had just graduated from high school and was getting ready to start his freshman year at college. His oldest had just graduated from college.

"I can't imagine them as anything but little kids," I said, shaking my head.

His eyes met mine. "You've been gone a long time."

I frowned. He was right. Sometimes my former life in San Francisco felt like a dream and other times, like seeing Kato again, it felt like yesterday.

Hair damp around my face from my sweaty workout, I grabbed my hoodie and headed for the door.

"I expect you here tomorrow at six."

"At night?"

"Ha ha, Gia. A.M."

I nodded. "Deal. Only if you let me take you and Susie out to dinner soon."

"Deal," he said and smiled back. Just then, a half dozen students rushed past me, coming up the stairs into the Dojo. They were all speaking at once. I gave Kato a salute and jogged down the stairs, even though my thighs were killing me.

My phone dinged.

Dante.

"Your attorney called. It's not good. Thank god you're staying at Darling's place for a few days."

Oh fuck.

"Um, I'm actually back in the city."

"Jesus."

I cringed.

"You need to turn around and go back there right now."

"I was just at the dojo with Kato. My car's at the hotel."

"Don't go back to the hotel. They just had a squad parked out front. I'm pretty damn sure it's for you."

Alarm zinged through me. "So, there is an arrest warrant?"

"Not yet. They called your attorney. They want you to stay in town. And he thinks they want to pick you up and put some more pressure on you. Keep you for as long as they can without actually arresting you. Squeeze you. Try to get you to confess."

"Good fucking luck."

"Unless you want to spend the next twenty-four hours in a little interview room, I suggest you call Tony and ask him to drive you back to Marin County. After you call him, turn off your phone. Call me from Darling's landline when you get there."

Motherfucker.

28

I hated to run back to Darlings, but I also didn't want to get picked up and questioned again. Especially not for hours at a time. So for once, I did what Dante said.

Tony didn't seem to mind the drive.

"Good to get away a bit on the open road," he said.

I made a face. "Are you sure? You're not just saying that?"

"Scout's honor."

We made it to Darling's in record time.

"You need me to wait for you?"

I leaned over and kissed his grizzled cheek. "I'm good. Drive home safe, my friend. Thank you."

He actually turned red.

"I got you, Gia."

"I know."

Then I was at the front door, knocking instead of ringing Darling's doorbell. I didn't want to wake the whole house if she was still asleep. She did like to sleep in.

She answered the door herself, dressed in a long, silky robe with a fur collar and hem. But her makeup was flawless.

"Good Lordie, it's early Gia. Didn't you just leave here anyway?"

"Dante's being paranoid. Told me to come back here and then call him from your landline."

"Looks like little Gia is all grown up. There once was a time you didn't listen to another damn soul. Now you're getting smarter. You know we all boss you around for your own good."

I decided not to tell her that he hadn't wanted me to go back to the city in the first place.

"Ha ha," I said and followed her in.

"I'm having my tea in the sunroom. There's fresh coffee, too. Grab a mug and meet me in the sunroom. I have a phone in there," she turned. "Unless you need some privacy."

"I just barged into your home. I think you can listen to the reason why."

She laughed.

I poured a cup of coffee in her giant kitchen and then made my way into the sunroom where her dogs were curled up on giant plush cushions.

"Some watchdogs they are," I said. "They didn't even notice me come in."

"Ring the damn doorbell, and you'll have another experience altogether."

"Note to self."

I gulped half of my coffee and dialed Dante.

"Yo."

One of the dogs came over and sat right on my foot. I made a face.

"That means she loves you," Darling said.

I reached down and scratched the dog's ears. I had to admit I liked the attention from the dog. I missed owning a dog more than I could say.

"Detective Stone called your attorney and said that you need to stay in town. We told him it was too late and you were already out of town."

"Good."

"I don't know what else is going on. Keep your phone off. For now. I think the best strategy until we find out more is to have you unavailable. That way you aren't breaking any laws or disregarding orders from the detective. I'm sorry. I didn't know how else to handle it."

"So, does this mean I can skip the gala?"

The gala was in two nights.

"We'll see."

Darling raised her eyebrow.

"Darling says hello," I said. 'You're on speakerphone."

"Hey beautiful," he said.

Darling's face spread into a huge smile.

"Dante, I do love you, you know."

"The feeling's mutual sweetie."

She took a sip of her tea and batted her eyelashes even though nobody could see her. Such a diva.

"Enough of your love fest," I said, rolling my eyes. "What do you think they have on me? Besides that video of a woman who clearly is not me. I would never wear those shoes with that outfit."

"That's what I said," Dante said. "I told James that."

I was quiet for a few seconds. "What did he say?"

"He was the one who brought it up. He said he didn't think you'd wear them."

Somebody was trying to imitate me but had failed. I didn't think I needed to be too worried about a real murder charge sticking.

"What else, that fake-ass video?"

"I told you, that's what we're going to find out. Sit tight. Don't turn on your phone. I don't want anyone to be able to reach you.

I'll call you there tomorrow morning."

I swallowed. "Dante? Should I be worried?"

He didn't answer for a few seconds. Then he cleared his throat.

"I really don't know."

———

Darling and I stayed up late with our feet curled up under us on her plush velvet couches, drinking red wine, eating chocolate, and reminiscing about the good old days when she owned the most popular hair salon in San Francisco.

It was a small community unto itself, and she had been the queen.

She had a back office where she ran her "other" business.

Women in abusive relationships would knock on her door in the back room and plead their cases. Darling provided them with new identities and falsified documents such as birth certificates, driver's licenses, social security cards so they could start a new life away from their abusers. She also gave them some seed money to get started.

It wasn't long before she had more money than she knew what to do with, and she invested in property around the Bay Area. A few years back, she sold her salon to the daughter of a good friend, turned over her false ID business to the woman, as well, and moved permanently to her Marin County home.

Here, she set up shop as an angel investor, working to help women and minorities flourish. But she was like the people on Shark Tank—you had to have a damn good business plan or a really hard luck case along with the drive and conviction to convince her to back you.

If she thought you were scrappy, she'd help you get your business idea off the ground.

I loved her for this.

After catching up on all the years we'd been apart, we both went to bed in the early hours of the morning.

When I woke, I rolled over to check my phone but remembered that Dante was going to call me on the landline. I pulled a soft sweater over my silk camisole and shorts and then padded into the kitchen in my socks.

All was quiet.

I found a pot of coffee in a stainless steel carafe and a note from Darling saying she was in town until early afternoon and to make myself at home.

I took my coffee out to the pool. It faced the east and was bathed in warm sunlight.

As soon as I'd settled into the lounge chair I heard the phone ring in the house. *Damn it!*

I sprinted inside and grabbed it. "Darling's place."

"It's me."

Dante. Thank God.

"I spoke to the attorney. He doesn't think they have enough to arrest you, so you should be safe to come back to the city. He said if they want you to come in, he'll accompany you, but it can't be until tomorrow. He's in court today."

"What if I don't want to talk to them tomorrow either?" I asked. I began opening cupboards, looking for something to eat. For a woman with Darling's healthy appetites, there was very little edible in her cupboards. Some weird protein powder canisters and Kombucha jars and some funky-ass Scandinavian crackers. I plucked a cracker out and stuck it in my mouth. I spit it out. It had the consistency of cardboard and tasted worse.

"You can talk to him about that. You two have a meeting at ten tomorrow morning. He'll come to the hotel."

"Fine," I said. This was all such a pain in the ass. I opened the refrigerator door. The inside looked more promising.

"I just picked up your dress."

"Say what?" I said, grabbing a bag of onion bagels out of the refrigerator. Score. If I could find some lox, cream cheese, and capers...

"For the gala."

"Oh fuck." I'd tried to forget about the gala.

"I couldn't decide between black velvet, red silk, or white satin."

He paused dramatically. I rolled my eyes.

"I'm holding my breath," I said sarcastically.

"At first, I thought the red silk," he said triumphantly. "With your black hair? Mama mia!"

"Isn't red a little, I don't know, flashy?" I had searched every inch of the refrigerator and there was no cream cheese. Ridiculous.

"It's a gala, Gia. Flashy is good. All the other women are going to be wearing as fancy as they can. They'll probably break out all the family jewels. That's why you're not wearing any."

"No jewelry? Cool." I honestly could give a fuck. I hated to admit it, but I wondered what that opera diva was going to wear. The woman James was going to marry. Ugh.

"But I decided against the red and against the jewels."

"Do tell," I said and stuck the bagel slices in a toaster I found on a bottom shelf in a cupboard.

"You are going to wear a black velvet dress."

"K," I said. I took out some butter thinking, *What kind of house has bagels without cream cheese?*

"You'll wear it with your Louboutin stilettos and no jewelry except the ring that Nico gave you."

"Perfect," I said, eyeing the toaster oven as my stomach grumbled.

"But you are going to wear the reddest lipstick I can find," he said. "That will be the final touch."

"I'm down for that," I said.

"You might not want to eat today."

"Fuck that," I said watching the bagel turn brown through the oven's little window.

"The velvet dress is formfitting and backless. It's simple, sexy, and elegant."

"I love you, Dante."

"I know."

"You just love me because I'm your real life dress-up Italian Barbie."

"Guilty as charged."

"When can I come home and start getting ready?" I said, peering out the front of Darling's house.

"Tony should be there any minute. I called him earlier."

"I better run," I said.

After I hung up with Dante and scarfed down my bagel, I wrote Darling a note.

"Next time I host you at the hotel. Spa day, baby. Love you."

By the time I brushed my teeth and threw my things in a bag, Tony was out front.

We listened to Otis Redding and James Brown all the way back.

We had the sort of comfortable relationship where we didn't need to fill the silence with needless chatter, but when he pulled up in front of the hotel, he turned to me.

"Everything okay, boss lady?"

I smiled. "I think so. I didn't kill anybody. At least not the people they're saying I killed."

He nodded solemnly. There were no secrets between me and him.

We'd both seen the dark side of life and that was part of our bond.

I smiled at him and patted his grizzled cheek. "You are a prince among men," I said.

He cleared his throat and I paused, my hand on the door handle. He usually avoided mushy conversations, but he obviously had something to say.

"I left my violent life behind a long time ago, as you know. But there are a handful of people in this world I'd kill for. And you should know you're one of them."

I felt tears prick my eyes.

"I feel the same way, Tony."

29

When I got up to my room, the black velvet dress was hanging in the front of my closet. I would have to talk to management about coming in my room. I didn't like it one bit. I quickly looked over at my laptop. I'd placed a hair strategically on the keyboard, so when I closed the lid, it stuck out a bit. The hair was still there. Good thing.

I wouldn't abide people snooping through my stuff.

I wasn't worried about the regular employees at the hotel. I was worried about someone in management using delivery of my clothes as an excuse to snoop in my room. As far as I knew nobody was wise to the investigation but Dante and I, but you just never knew.

Since I had a few hours to kill, I decided to look at my top three suspects. It was a way to distract myself from thinking about the cops investigating me.

Even though Maxwell Carlton was dead, that didn't mean he was no longer a suspect in the embezzlement. In fact, hearing he'd made a bid to buy the hotel made him even more of a suspect in my book.

I had to carry on and pretend that there wasn't a possible murder charge in my future. If I didn't, I'd go crazy.

All three of the dead men had access to the hotel books. They all dealt with various aspects of the hotel's financials. And, based on the background information Danny had sent me, it appeared all three of them had good motives to steal.

Maxwell Carlton might have been stealing money from the hotel to buy the hotel. Odd but possible. It was enough for him to put a down payment on the property and get a loan for the rest.

Stuart McBride, the food and beverage director, had recently divorced his wife and had been ordered by the court to pay some hefty alimony. His four kids were all in private school.

Cynthia Turner, the hotel maintenance engineer, had just bought a house that, frankly, seemed a little out of her paygrade. The bank records showed she'd put down a hefty deposit on the loan. Sure, she could've saved that much, but it seemed like a lot. Plus, the new monthly mortgage amount wasn't anything to sneeze at.

After pouring over this for two hours, I finally shut my laptop and hopped in the shower.

I didn't want to be rushed getting ready for the gala. It started at 9:00 p.m. I wanted to shower and then take a long nap before I had to finish getting ready.

I crawled into bed naked with my hair wet from the shower. When I woke up, it was sunset. I was horny, but resisted the urge to call Ryder for more phone sex. Maybe tonight I'd take on the mayor. *Nah.* That was a very bad idea.

I was a grown-ass woman. I could control my sexual urges, right? Right?

I hopped up and caught a glance of myself in the mirror.

My hair had dried into beachy waves, and I decided to keep it that way for the night.

I'd have a drink, do my makeup, and get dressed right before Dante was supposed to arrive.

Wearing underwear and a tank top, I headed to my living room. There, I lounged on the couch and poured some tequila. That's one thing I loved about the hotel suite—the full bar. The drink hit the spot. I hoped it would tide me over until the gala.

Despite myself, I was a little excited about the gala. I didn't want to admit that I was looking forward to seeing James again. If I was smart, I'd try to avoid him at all costs. *Damn it.*

Thinking this, I downed my tequila and poured another. It burned my throat and warmed my belly, and I lay back, taking in the view of the Golden Gate as the sun set on it.

I was lonely.

I felt like I'd been lonely my entire life. It's true there was a brief period with Nico when I didn't feel this way, especially when Rose was young. For that time, I felt like part of a family.

But here I was alone again.

Sure, I had my created my own family over the years—Dante, Darling, Danny—but they all had their own full lives now.

I wonder what Freud would say about my tendency to attract friends with names that started with a "D?" It was fucking strange. Even our dogs: Django and now Rose with Dylan.

Ryder was an exciting and dangerous lover, but he lived in the South of France. Sure, he could visit, or I could go see him, but we weren't going to have any real relationship.

Me and James? It's complicated. We both knew we could never be together again. Even if Madame Butterfly wasn't in the picture. Then why did I feel such a pull toward him? It sucked.

I needed a distraction so I'd quit obsessing over getting James into bed. It was starting to be annoying. I thought about the mayor again. Hot. But also, way too dangerous.

As the alcohol warmed me from the inside out, I realized

that if I didn't stop thinking about getting laid right then, I was going to do something crazy.

I reached for my phone and found a playlist I'd made on the airplane. It connected to the Bluetooth speakers in the hotel suite, and I cranked it up and danced around to some old-school rap.

After a while, I realized it was dark outside and time to start getting ready.

I did my makeup first.

Despite my childish urges to ignore Dante, I took his advice and kept my makeup simple—black mascara on my eyelashes, just a little black eyeliner, and then full-on blood red lipstick. I pouted at myself in the mirror. It would work.

I pulled the dress on. It glided across my body like silk. The neckline was straight across but draped slightly revealing a large swath of my chest and collarbone without showing any cleavage. It followed the contours of my waist and hips and then fell straight to the floor in a pool of black softness. The back was the showstopper. It was bare all the way down to where the fabric hugged my ass. It almost, but not quite, dipped too low, stopping just in time. The dress was the softest, silkiest velvet I'd ever touched. It felt delicious against my bare skin.

Dante had been right. No jewelry except Nico's ring.

I slipped it on and closed my eyes for a second, allowing myself to think of Nico the first time we made love.

We were enemies at the time. I'd been stalking him at a deserted beach on the Mexican coast, intent on assassinating him. He was trying to take away Rose, who, although she was his biological daughter, was more my child than his at the time.

Alone in his beach house with his bodyguards dismissed, we had wild sex in his kitchen. It was the first time I'd experienced the prowess of an older man, and it had rocked my world. I'd known in that moment that for the first time in my life, I'd met my match in the drug cartel leader. With hindsight, I think I fell in love with him that first night even though it took us both a while to figure out we were meant to be together—until death parted us.

I realized I was staring in the mirror at myself in the dress imagining him coming up behind me and kissing my bare back. I shivered. It had felt like he was there with me. Impossible.

I scooped up a small bag with a chain strap and my stilettos and headed into the living room. I turned off all the lights and poured another tequila. I found a crumpled pack of cigarettes and headed out to the deck. There, leaning over the railing looking at San Francisco, I drank my tequila and smoked a cigarette.

I was an on-and-off smoker over the years. After Nico died, I was no longer as concerned about my health and began smoking more again. It was sad but true. I had less to live for nowadays. Even Rose no longer needed me.

I was lost in thought when I heard a knock on the door.
Dante.
I stubbed out my cigarette and downed my drink.
Time to play good girl.

30

The Gala

I WAS DYING FOR A CIGARETTE.

But the senator standing before me in his tuxedo droned on about his pancreatitis and how he could only drink top shelf bourbon or he'd end up in the hospital or something.

Yawn.

I tried not be obvious as I glanced over his shoulder at the rest of the chandelier-lit room. The backdrop on four sides was the San Francisco skyline at night—one of my favorite views in the world.

Although the music at the gala was low and sultry, the clink of Champagne glasses and rustle of silk and taffeta and the murmur of drunken voices made it difficult for me to hear what the senator was saying.

And that was just fine by me.

I was sort of zoning out, thinking that maybe instead of a cigarette I could rustle up a joint from one of the cute waiters. I tried to make eye contact with one who looked like he might have some weed on him. He was dressed in the required black button-down shirt and black slacks, but something about him was laissez faire. Maybe it was his hair, longer than the other waiters, or the slight scruff under his lower lip, or the tattoo that snaked around his wrist that gave him such a bad-boy air.

I caught his eye as he headed to the kitchen with a tray full of empty glasses. He did a double take and then slowly looked me up and down before smiling.

It made me feel like a pervert.

Was he even eighteen?

I knew I didn't look my age in my black dress and stilettos, but even if I knocked off a few years, I could be his mother.

I silently sent him a message: *I'm not trying to fuck you, I just want your drugs.*

At that point, I became obsessed with getting high to make it through the evening, so I wasn't really very focused when the senator leaned in and repeated a question I apparently hadn't heard.

I backed up. His breath was atrocious.

Over his shoulder, I saw another VIP making a beeline for me.

Everyone wanted to talk to me tonight.

The senator was the fourth dignitary to waylay me.

For the millionth time, I tried to catch Dante's eye, but he was deep in conversation with the head of the Chamber of Commerce. *Shit.* It was all Dante's fault I was here. He owed me big time.

My scalp tingled a little bit, and I turned to see Nicoletta Marchese looking at me. She tossed her strawberry blonde hair and gave me a smile before turning away, leaning down toward James's wheelchair to whisper something in his ear.

My face burned.

Obviously, she'd wanted me to see.

I swallowed back the lump of jealousy. That ship had sailed years ago. He was no longer mine and never would be again. Despite what had happened.

But he was too good for her.

There was something about the willowy opera singer that made me wary.

It wasn't her fake-as-fuckness. It was something else. Something darker and more sinister.

Oliver Kingsley Hollingsworth, one of the richest men in San Francisco—and frankly one of the oldest—sidled up to her with his boy toy. Both men were gay, but that didn't stop the old geezer from caressing Nicoletta's shiny taffeta-clad ass as he went in for hugs and cheek kisses. Who knew the old boy was AC/DC?

Then the boy toy, Charles Wellington, whispered something in Nicoletta's ear. She laughed and then leaned over and kissed Old Oliver smack dab on the mouth. He gave a gruff laugh but reached out and groped her waist, pressing her up against him. What the fuck?

Were they propositioning her? Come to think of it, Dante had mentioned Hollingsworth was into some kinky shit. Dude was rich enough to pay for any depraved sex act he wanted. There were some crazy stories about the things he liked to stick his dick into. Whatever. To each their own. I just wondered if James knew what his girlfriend was up to.

I shook my head. Poor James. His wheelchair had been turned away during the whole encounter. He didn't have a clue. If that dumb bitch broke his heart, I'd kill her.

But right now, he wasn't my problem. And she wasn't worth my time or energy.

After tonight, I hoped to never see her again.

In fact, I hoped to never see 99 percent of the people in the room again. But that was just a pipe dream.

As a waiter passed, I scooped another glass of champagne off his tray and downed it.

"Miss Santangelo?"

Beatrice Stanford, a retired opera singer who liked to regale everyone with stories of her glory days, was at my side.

"It's Santella."

"Isabella?"

I gave up.

"Just call me Gia."

She cleared her throat and started over.

"Miss Gia, where is your partner, Dante?" She was looking over my shoulder. "I thought we had agreed that the salmon canapes wouldn't contain capers. They keep rolling off onto the floor."

She'd been on the board for the gala, but as far as I knew hadn't done a damn thing except give her opinion about everything and anything.

I shifted to look past her. Sure enough, there were little green balls on the carpet. Oops.

"Not sure," I said. "But I don't think Dante was in charge of the food, was he?"

I plastered a smile on my face.

As I looked over her shoulder, I made eye contact with the mayor. He was heading my way, trying to make his way through the crowd.

Shit.

The mayor had a hot nut for me since we met. We'd been on one date. It was fine. Not even a kiss goodnight. It was for the best.

In the old days, I would've fucked him in a heartbeat. But now, he made me want to run far and fast away. He was good looking, intelligent, powerful, compassionate, and funny.

In other words, dangerous as fuck.

"Excuse me!" I said to Beatrice Stanford and fled toward the kitchen.

I rushed through the swinging double doors and let out a huge over-the-top sigh.

The staff, a cook, and a few waiters looked startled.

"Sorry," I said, looking for the dark-haired waiter.

He was in the back, slouched against the wall near two other waiters. They were smoking vapes. I knew what was inside the cartridges. My instincts had been right.

I pointed my finger at him and crooked it.

He pushed himself off the wall, and his friends shoved him and made snide comments.

When he got in front of me, he gave me a cocky grin.

To my surprise, he was taller than me. And even better looking close up. He exuded an animalistic sensuality. His eyes bored through me.

"At your service, Ms. Santella."

I was a little surprised he knew who I was, but didn't say anything.

Instead, I met his eyes. He licked his lips. I stared at his lips. Fuck. He was a baby. How could I look at him that way? I quickly looked away.

"I need your vape."

He grinned. "Oh yeah?"

"Yeah."

"Well, I only brought enough to get me and my boys through this night. It's all gone."

Oh, he *was* a cocky one, wasn't he?

"I'll make it worth your while," I said, my eyes narrowing.

"How you gonna do that?" he said, and his eyes roamed my body. "I don't need your money."

"You like your job here?" I cocked my head.

He frowned.

Shit. I'd pissed him off.

"Listen. I'm just asking for a favor here. If you could hook me up with something to get me through this god-awful night, I'd appreciate it. I'd owe you. I'd owe you a favor. I don't give favors lightly."

"Is it that bad out there?" he said, jutting his chin toward the ball room.

I sighed. "What do you think? I've got a bunch of rich fucks who think because they paid a small fortune to be here they get to tell me about their fucking bunions and stomach ulcers. Normally I would tell them to fuck off, but since I'm on the board...and it's for a good cause." I paused. "I have to at least be polite. It's killing me."

He nodded.

"I need to go get my stash. It's in the car. Meet me on the roof in fifteen minutes."

The last time I'd arranged to meet someone on the roof, I'd arrived to find him dead.

"Fine," I said reluctantly.

I watched him go and, despite myself, admired his long, lean body and his muscled forearms. At the last minute, he turned and caught me checking him out. My cheeks grew hot. I felt like a fucking pervert. Ugh.

As soon as I stepped out of the kitchen, I saw Dante across the room.

He was talking to James.

That's when I had to admit to myself the real reason I wanted to be drunk and high. I didn't want to face James.

Not after what had happened.

On the plane back to San Francisco from Indonesia two weeks ago, I had thought about all the people I loved who I might see again. When I thought of James, I felt a warm, nostalgic bond. I had thought my feelings for him were gone.

After all, we had broken up so very long ago. He had a new life with a wife and kids.

I would always love him, but it would no longer hurt to see him.

Oh, how wrong I had been.

I had been away a long time. And a lot had changed.

He was now a widower. And someone's boyfriend.

Now, seeing him talking to Dante was like a knife in the heart.

Again.

I was regressing. Both men stopped talking and looked over at me. My heart stuttered. Then they said something and laughed.

I heard a voice say, "Gia Santella! There you are. I've been looking for you for the past hour."

Of course he had.

It was another dude from the gala board who always stared at my tits.

But instead of wanting to run away, I now felt relief.

I turned and gave him a brilliant smile, turning toward him and placing him in front of me so he blocked my view of Dante and James.

The last thing I saw before his big head took over everything was Nicoletta in her white dress with the ugly-ass mermaid tail hem sidling up to James and putting a protective hand on the back of his wheelchair. She was staring at me with a smug fucking look the entire time.

Time to bail.

"Excuse me," I said. "I have to use the ladies room." I headed for the exit.

"Wait," I heard him say behind me. "The restrooms are the other way."

But then I slipped outside and opened the door to the stairs with my employee key card.

At the top of the stairs, the door to the roof was propped open. As I neared it, the first thing I saw was a midnight blue sky full of twinkling stars—a rare sight in San Francisco, which often had a glowing, orange night sky.

I stepped out and inhaled deeply. The air smelled like a combination of salt from the ocean breeze and the fresh greenness of forest, maybe blown over from Marin County.

Suddenly the waiter was in front of me.

Thank God. I was done with finding dead bodies for a lifetime.

He grabbed me and kissed me, pressing me back against the wall. I planted my palms on his chest and pushed him away. Hard. He was lucky I didn't demolish his balls with my knee.

"What the fuck?" I said.

"I saw the way you looked at me."

"You're just a kid," I said, not denying his words.

"I'm twenty-three."

"Like I said, 'a kid.'" But he was older than I'd thought. He actually couldn't be my son. Thank god. I'd been feeling like a pervert for the way I looked at him earlier.

"You're so sexy," he said, his hands on my waist, drawing me closer. "Let me show you how sexy I think you are."

"Where's your vape? I asked. But inwardly I groaned. His lower body pressed against mine, and I could feel his hardness and it made any resolve I had melt away.

I hadn't had sex for a long time. Since Ryder in Barcelona. That seemed like a lifetime ago. And before that, when Nico was still alive but in the care home, I went without sex for years. It was ridiculous. Sex was healthy.

I loved sex. I wanted sex. Once upon a time, I didn't even

think twice about having sex with a stranger. In fact, I took pride in it.

We took turns smoking his vape. It was some damn good weed. Top notch stuff.

He handed me a joint. "You can have this for later. To remember me."

Aw, he was cute.

He leaned back toward me, his face before mine, his eyes trained on my mouth. Then his lips were on my neck.

"I think this is a bad idea," I said. Even I recognized it as the feeble protest it was.

"I don't believe you," he said in a low, husky voice. "I don't believe for one second you buy into that sexist double standard. Men can be with younger women, but women can't be with a younger guy? That's total crap."

He had a point.

His mouth was working its way up my neck. One of his hands was still firm on my waist. His other hand wrapped around the back of my neck, tangled in my hair. His breath was heavy now and I matched it. The anticipation of another kiss was irresistible. All logic and reason fled my mind. My body took over.

I could feel the heat coming off of him in waves. He leaned forward, his mouth was on mine, and despite myself I groaned in pleasure. And it just got better from there.

After, I pulled the hem of my dress back down as he buttoned up his pants.

"Holy shit," he said, still breathless.

I exhaled loudly. "Okay, maybe it actually was a really good idea."

He pulled me close and kissed me again. I let him.

Then he drew back.

"I gotta go," he said, looking over his shoulder, but still

holding onto my waist. "Do you think maybe one day..."

He trailed off. He already knew the answer.

I shook my head.

Then he was gone, back down the stairs.

I walked over to the edge of the roof and looked down at the city below me.

I'd lived around the world, but this city would always be my compass point, my ground zero, my homing beacon.

Even though I'd grown up in Monterey, I hadn't felt like myself until I moved to San Francisco after my parent's murder.

It would always be home.

I rummaged around in my bag and found my pack cigarettes and gunmetal Zippo lighter.

I pulled the joint the waiter had given me from the pack, lit it, and inhaled deeply, savoring the flavor and instant feeling of mellow gold that suffused my entire body.

At first, I was more annoyed than anything when I heard voices and the door open up behind me.

I didn't turn around. I hoped if I ignored whomever it was, they'd go away.

Then I heard the squawk of a police radio. I couldn't make out what it said.

I froze.

"Gia Santella?" a deep voice said.

Cold fear trickled through me. "Yes?"

"You're under arrest."

At first, it didn't register. Then I thought about the boy I'd been with only moments before. He'd told me he was twenty-three. And pot was legal now in California...

It took a second for me to register the rest of what the police officer had said.

"You're under arrest *for murder*."

31

CHARLES WATCHED WITH HOODED EYES AS THE UNIFORMED POLICE officers stepped out of the elevator into the restaurant. Most of the well-dressed and half-sauced crowd didn't notice their arrival. But Charles did.

He'd been the one to call them and tell them Gia Santella was at the party.

Shortly after they arrived James had received a call that an arrest warrant had been issued for Gia. Nicoletta had overheard the conversation in the elevator. She immediately texted Charles.

Then, when they arrived in the restaurant, Charles was standing near Nicoletta and James when Gia stepped out of the elevator.

"Shouldn't we call 911?" Nicoletta had said to James.

He'd looked at her like she was crazy. Then he had turned his wheelchair to face someone else and struck up a conversation.

Nicoletta was ashen faced.

Charles was humiliated for her. He wanted to strangle the

stupid cop. How dare he treat her like that. Nicoletta glanced over at him and Charles held up his cell phone.

She gave a sly smile.

Charles dipped into a corner and dialed 911.

Now the cops scanned the crowded room. Beatrice Stanford was closest to them. They approached her and said something that made her fling a bejeweled hand up to her mouth. Then she pointed at a door.

Less than five minutes later, the officers emerged with Gia Santella between them.

She was handcuffed. She held her head high and her eyes were straight ahead.

Damn. She was a force.

Suddenly, Charles wished he'd handled the entire thing differently.

He wanted to see what she was like in bed.

Probably the exact opposite of Nicoletta.

Gia Santella was probably a wild cat.

Now, he'd never know.

When he looked up, he saw Nicoletta watching him from across the room. She was facing the elevator. James was facing her so he couldn't see what had stopped conversation. The crowd parted as the officers led Gia Santella toward the elevator.

When he saw Nicoletta, guilt suffused him.

He tried to justify his lust for Gia. He shouldn't feel guilty about that.

Until he and Nicoletta left San Francisco they each shared another's bed.

He was fucking Old Man Hollingsworth and Nicoletta was boning that gimp cop. But those liaisons were all a means to an end.

For their plan to work, they needed a police commander in

their corner and they needed an inroad to Hollingsworth and his millions.

Nicoletta raised a delicate eyebrow as the police paraded Gia Santella to the elevator.

James finally seemed to get wind of what was going on and his wheelchair whirled 180 degrees in time for him to view the elevator doors closing with his ex-girlfriend inside.

So sad. Too fucking bad, Charles thought.

He was suddenly filled with pure hatred for the good-looking cop.

The man was not only fucking the woman he loved, but he had fucked the woman he lusted after. Some motherfuckers had all the luck.

But that was about to change.

If Charles knew one thing in life it was that he was responsible for creating his own luck.

And Gia Santella's arrest was nearly the last piece in the puzzle.

32

The San Francisco jail smelled like piss, sweat, and stale alcohol.

They stripped me, frisked me, and then shoved me in a small room with a glass panel in the door. At first, I pressed my face to the glass trying to see something—anything—but there just a blank wall across from me. I could hear other people grumbling in other rooms nearby.

At least I wasn't in some concrete-floored cell with a bunch of drug dealers and prostitutes. As the hours passed, I thought, then again, maybe that wouldn't be so bad. At least I'd have someone to talk to.

I was slumped in the corner asleep when the door finally opened. I had no idea how many hours later it was, but suspected it was close to noon the next day since my stomach was grumbling.

I stood and brushed the lint and dirt from the floor off my dress.

It was my attorney. He was boring looking. Gray hair. Gray suit. Gray complexion. He must never leave the inside of a court room. I didn't care what he looked like. I wanted him to make sure I never stepped foot inside a jail cell again.

He handed me a card. He didn't bother to greet me.

"They have a video of you killing Maxwell Carlton. It's you. Your face. The whole works."

"So, I heard," I said dryly. "It's not me."

He shrugged.

"Come on; you made bail," he said. "Your cop friend somehow convinced the judge to grant it and Dante paid it. There was a hell of an argument in chambers about it. The district attorney is usually a much more reasonable fellow, but he seems to have a dog in this hunt. I'm not sure why, but it's not good. He's going to do whatever it takes to make sure the charges stick and there is a conviction."

Then the attorney went on to say the judge released me under house arrest to James. I had to stay at his place.

Shit. That was a mistake.

I frowned. What was James up to?

"I've got a friend working to expose the technology that created the video. It's called Deepfake. Look it up. I'm going to need you to build a motherfucking watertight defense case for me based on flaws in that technology just in case I don't find the real killer first."

He paused and looked at me.

"I never lose," he said.

I looked right back at him and said, "Neither, do I."

We locked eyes and he gave a slow nod.

That's right, motherfucker, don't you dare underestimate me. This is the real deal.

My life and freedom is on the line here.

As we made our way to the lobby, I saw him through the glass panel in the door before he saw me.

James.

33

As soon as the door to his apartment closed behind us, I raced for the shower.

When I was done, I came out to find James waiting for me in the bedroom. I walked over and let the towel drop.

He pulled me onto his lap. I wasn't surprised. The heat between us had been pure fire as we drove from the jail to his place. There was an urgency there I didn't understand and didn't question.

The contact of our bodies sent a pulse of fiery desire through me. I turned to face him, my knees bent and my legs straddling him. I ran my fingers through his hair, letting my fingernails race over his scalp. My eyes never left his. They were dark pools of desire. He groaned.

"James..." I began.

He put his mouth on mine before I could continue. It was as if we'd never been apart. Our bodies responded as if they were one.

I'd forgotten how hot the chemistry between us had always been. James knew how to touch me in ways that drove me wild. He knew my body better than almost anyone ever had. Nico was the exception. It was different with Nico and I because our lovemaking was infused with such intense emotion—insane soulmate-type love stuff—that the physical aspect almost took a backseat to us expressing our deep, all-encompassing love for one another.

With James, the love was there, but it was less the focus. With James, it was truly about the physical act itself, striving for intense heights of pleasure.

Then we were in his bed with the black leather headboard. I lost track of time, completely outside my head and entirely in my body.

When we were done, I snuggled up to him and put my head on his shoulder. He absentmindedly ran his fingers through my hair. I sighed contentedly.

And then I blew it. With my big mouth.

"You know, if we got married, you couldn't testify against me in court."

He instantly grew stiff.

"I was just joking. Obviously neither one of us ever want to get married again."

He didn't answer. I glanced over. He was working the inside of his lip the way he always did when he was worried.

I sat up on one elbow. "Spill it."

"You know I'm seeing Nicoletta."

I smirked. "Yeah, she's a piece of work."

He frowned. "She's not that bad. She's been through a lot."

I flopped back on the pillow and shrugged even though I knew he wasn't looking.

"She's not in your league," I said. "Not even fucking close."

"I care about her."

I sat up. This wasn't good. "Is there something you're trying to tell me?" I asked, flinging my legs over the side of the bed. I was done with talking about Nicoletta while I lay naked with James. "You feeling guilty about tonight?"

He pulled himself to sitting. "Yeah. I guess I am. We probably shouldn't have done this. For so many reasons."

"Does she know you bailed me out and are vouching for me?"

He didn't answer.

"I'll take that as a no. Hey, relax," I said as I pulled on my lacy thong. "You guys aren't married. You're still a free agent."

Again, he didn't respond. I started to feel a sense of dread.

I turned to face him. His eyes flickered over my bare breasts and I saw the lust already there again. Who was he trying to fool? It was irritating.

"What's your point, James?"

"I just don't want you to think that...you know...me and you..."

He trailed off.

It stung. I felt my heart harden and lashed out angrily.

"Grow a pair, James," I said. "This means nothing to me. I knew what it was as soon as you kissed me. Two consenting adults. I don't expect anything else from you. In fact, I don't want anything else from you. Not even to stay here. I'll leave."

"You can't. I promised the judge."

That's when I knew. I would be gone before morning. It had always been inevitable. I had to fight for myself. As always. I was the only one I could count on to solve this problem. I couldn't stay with James and wait for him to find the real killer. It was up to me. And I couldn't do it locked up in this apartment.

I stared at him for a long moment.

"Gia," he said in a softer tone, "I just didn't want to lead you on. It's my fault. As soon as I saw you and realized you were back in town, I knew...I knew what would happen."

"So, what's the problem?" I said, searching for my bra on the floor until I remembered I hadn't been wearing one.

James was now dressed and had slid into his wheelchair. "The problem is, I'm seeing someone. I can't be with you."

I glared at him. "Let me make this perfectly clear. I don't want us to be together."

I was pissed. How did this all go to hell so quickly?

"Let me go," I said half-heartedly. "I'll just leave. You obviously don't want me here. What will your girlfriend do if she finds out I'm staying here? She's going to flip her shit."

He ran a hand through his hair.

"Damn it," he said. "You can't leave. You're under house arrest."

"This was the worst idea ever," I said. I stood, naked except for my lacy thong. "What am I supposed to wear while I'm here? My velvet dress?"

He didn't answer, so I headed for his closet. I found a long-sleeve black T-shirt and some black cargo pants. I cinched a belt until they stayed up around my waist.

He watched me silently and then when I turned to face him, he said, "Why is it always like this with us, Gia?"

"I don't know, James," I said, my voice cold. "But I know that this is why we will never be together."

He sat there for a few seconds in silence. I waited, growing even more irritated. I didn't understand what the point of this conversation was. All I wanted to do was get the fuck out of there. It had been such a great night, but it had gone south so quickly. Part of me wanted to cry. Why had he ruined everything?

"Please don't," he said.

"Don't what?" I snapped.

"Be like this." He grabbed his keys off a small table. "I'm going to go get us some food for dinner."

"Be like what?" I said angrily. "You're the one who brought up all this bullshit, James, not me."

He sighed loudly. "You're right. I'm sorry."

I shrugged. "Go get us some food. I'm starved."

I made my way to the kitchen and stuck my head in the refrigerator. I found an open bottle of white wine and grabbed it.

Who opened a bottle of wine and didn't finish it? Probably Soprano Sally.

I poured a glass and took a sip. I was holding my breath, dying for him to leave. But he kept watching me. Was he suspicious? I downed the glass of wine and poured another.

"Since I'm stuck here, I hope you don't mind if I get shit-faced? Be sure to get more wine while you're out."

There, that should convince him.

My skin was practically crawling with the intense desire to get the fuck out of his apartment. I felt like a fool. His attitude had tarnished what had just happened.

Then he made a move I hadn't expected: He put his head in his hands and rubbed his eyes with his palms. I stared. *What the fuck?*

"You okay?" I asked.

He shook his head. My anger disappeared. "What is it?"

He exhaled loudly. "I've always hoped deep down inside that we could be together again someday." His voice was so sad that I reached for his hand. He clutched mine tightly. He wouldn't look at me. "But at the same time, I know we can't. I put all that shit on you just now."

"Yeah," I said, but my voice was soft. "You did."

He wasn't done, though. "I want you in my life always, but we both know that if we tried to make it work as a couple, we would drive each other crazy. It's just who we are."

"I'm not disagreeing," I said.

"Tonight happened because I knew it would be the last time

before..." he trailed off and an icy finger of fear rippled through me.

"Before what, James?" Before I was sent to prison for life? Before what?

"Nicoletta is pregnant. I'm going to propose."

I closed my eyes. There was the knife through my heart.

"Gia?"

I opened my eyes and stared at him coldly.

"Big deal," I said. "This was your last fling. You're making too big a deal over it."

"Don't be like this," he said.

He was looking at me with such uncertainty that I leaned down and hugged him tightly.

"James. What do you want me to say? Congratulations on being a daddy again. Hope you like being married to Madame Butterfly?"

"Stop."

"You and me? Nothing can ever take away the love we have for one another. I will love you until the day I die," I said. "But you're right, we just aren't good for one another. We need to make sure this never happens again because it makes things way too damn complicated."

"I love you, Gia. I just can't be with you," he said. "I swear, if I would've known you were coming back to San Francisco..."

"Please don't," I said.

He looked at me and slowly nodded.

"Go get us something to eat," I said. "And then find the killer because I don't think it's a good idea for us to live together. We both know what's going to happen."

James opened his front door. But then he paused.

"Gia? That video?"

I swallowed.

"I know how it looks," I said. "I swear it wasn't me."

I looked in his eyes and realized that he didn't believe me.

I'd thought I couldn't hurt anymore on this night. I was wrong.

"I don't know what to do," he said. "I want to believe you. I mean, I do believe you. But the video. It's you. It doesn't make any sense. Gia, I swear you can tell me anything. Even if you did it, we can get you help. We can figure this out. You just need to tell me what really happened that night."

My heart broke. He really didn't believe me. He waited and then his face filled with disappointment. He was waiting for a confession I didn't have to give.

Finally, he looked away. "Thai?"

"Sure," I said and kissed his cheek like the Judas I was. I turned away before he could see my face.

"No offense," he said. "But I'm going to set the alarm before I go."

I nodded without turning around. His suspicion and distrust made it easier to betray him.

As soon as the door closed, I raced to the bedroom. I found a thick black hoodie and some oversized military boots. I tugged them on. I found a backpack in the corner and quickly packed it with a few spare clothing items and one of James's guns from a shelf in his closet. I slung the straps over my back and raced toward the sliding glass doors leading to his deck.

Outside, I peered down on the street. It was too far to jump without breaking both my legs, but the deck on the floor below was closer. If I hung over the edge and dropped to that one I would be closer to the street. Still too far to jump...although...

I pulled myself over the edge and jumped to the deck below with a soft thud. I remained in a crouch for a second, eyes glued on the empty and dark apartment. When I realized nobody was home, I tried the sliding glass door. Unlocked. I crept through to the front door, holding my breath. Somebody could still be home in the dark apartment sleeping or something. But I made it to the front door and slipped out. Then I raced to the back stairwell and ran down the other two flights to the street. I cracked the door and looked out. James was long gone.

I stepped out into the cold night air and took a deep breath.

Here we go.

34

"I FIND IT NEXT TO IMPOSSIBLE TO BELIEVE THAT MS. SANTELLA murdered anyone, much less Maxwell Carlton," the mayor said into his phone as he paced the deck of his Russian Hill apartment.

The district attorney was spouting some nonsense in his ear about motive—something to do with Carlton and Gia both wanting to buy the hotel.

"Nonsense," Anthony Ferraro said. "I spoke with the owner a few minutes ago. Carlton made an offer and was immediately turned down. The owner has already agreed to sell to Ms. Santella and her partner. It wasn't about the money. Herr Janson is richer than dirt, Chief. He doesn't care about money. He wanted to sell the hotel to someone he likes. And he doesn't like —or didn't like—Carlton. In fact, he suspects him of embezzling from the hotel."

Ferraro paced more as he listened to the DA go on.

Finally, he said, "My point is that there is no motive. Ms. Santella is an intelligent and quite rational woman. She wouldn't murder someone because they made an offer to buy a hotel she was already buying. The whole idea is utterly absurd. Even you have to admit that."

After another ten minutes arguing and getting nowhere, the mayor finally said, "Don't fuck this up, Woodman. Like me, you serve at the will of the people."

He hung up.

"I'm still baffled how that idiot ever got to the position he is in," he said to the small dog at his feet. "You'd do a better job, Rascal."

Ferraro picked up the phone again.

"Chief Sandoval, please."

When the chief got on the phone, there was the slightest moment of awkwardness before they both got over it. They'd dated briefly the previous summer and then decided to be friends instead.

"What can I do for you, Anthony?"

"I don't think Gia Santella is your perp."

"Strange that you're not the only one who has told me this lately," the chief said lightly. "I don't suppose your doubt has anything to do with the fact that she looks like an Italian movie star?"

"Does she?" he asked, immediately regretting playing dumb.

"There's a video of her killing Maxwell Carlton. What would you like me to do about it? I'm not an attorney, Anthony. I simply deal with facts. My detectives gathered enough evidence to convince Judge Proctor to issue an arrest warrant. What do you want me to do?"

"Your job," the mayor said. "She's not your perp. That means someone else out there is walking around scot-free."

"Anthony, my hands are tied."

"Thanks anyway," he said and hung up. So much for parting amiably. He was pretty sure he'd just royally pissed her off.

The mayor had one more call to make. The Attorney

General for the state of California. Merilee Conley. Another former girlfriend and lover. Thank God, he always ended his relationships on a good note.

"Merilee? I need your help. A woman I know is being framed with a video I would stake my life on not being her. But I've seen it with my own eyes. It's her. What the hell?"

Merilee had an answer—a ready answer. It was called Deepfake technology. She quickly explained it to the mayor.

"What can I do about it?" he asked.

Thirty minutes later the mayor had a game plan to try to help Gia Santella.

He shook his head. He didn't know why he was going to put his neck on the line for a woman he barely knew, but he'd never felt more compelled to do anything in his life.

35

SORRY, NOT SORRY, JAMES.

As soon as my feet hit the pavement, I ran.

My first stop was to buy three burner phones. I knew the camera in the store would capture my purchase, so I headed straight to the Tenderloin to buy them.

James and Dante and anyone else who knew me would think I retreated to my old neighborhood, but I had no plans to stay in the TL. Too obvious.

Instead, I headed for the docks. I knew there was a homeless community there.

I needed a vehicle to sleep in.

As soon as I got the first burner phone up and running, I dialed Tony.

"I need a van. No windows. I'm on the run. A murder rap. I didn't do it."

He didn't even hesitate.

"I'll have a van for you in the parking lot of El Mercado's Burritos in the Mission. Key will be on top of the passenger side rear tire. 0700."

Then he hung up.

I had an hour to kill.

I pulled my hair back in a tight ponytail and pulled my hoodie up until most of my face was obscured. I headed to Chinatown. I walked the streets, ducking my head to avoid any CCTV cameras.

Aware of the possibility that every camera in the city would eventually be searching for my face, I walked with my head down and hopped a bus headed toward the Mission.

I snuck into a bodega and bought a bag of food that wouldn't go bad—canned beans, tuna, bottled water, and some beef jerky. I wasn't sure how long I was going to have to hide out.

I'd lay low in the city—maybe pay someone to use my ID to get out of town. My only hope was to stay in town and figure out who was framing me. If I ran, I wouldn't be able to prove my innocence.

Speaking of, I needed help.

While I hid in the alley near the bodega I dialed Danny. He didn't pick up. He was probably still asleep. I left a message.

"I'm on the run. I'll call you in four hours."

That should give me enough time to settle into my new home at the homeless camp.

The van was where Tony said it would be. Of course. That guy was salt of the earth. I could count on him during the apocalypse. If he said he'd do something, you could count on it.

I drove over to the homeless camp and parked in a spot near the underpass. I knew the cops didn't come down there very often. During our dinner, the mayor had said helping the homeless was one of his top priorities, and that was one reason he told the cops to lay off this camp until the city had a better option for these people.

Once I was parked, I dialed Danny.

"Any luck? How do we fight back against this type of technology?" I asked.

"If you know what to look for, you might be able to tell a Deepfake," he said. "There's a whole list of stuff to look for. Are they blinking naturally, making weird faces, is their posture weird, are their movements jerky or disjointed? Is the lighting weird, like with shadows or their skin tone? Is the hair weird? Like you can't really recreate frizzy hair. When they smile, are their teeth just a line of white without individual teeth? Is it blurry? Are the voices weird or out of synch with the movement of the mouth?"

"Are all these things enough to prove its Deepfake?" I asked. "Like will this hold up in court?"

"I don't know. I know the first thing I did was slow down the video so I could look at it better. The problem is, it was filmed in the dark, so I couldn't really zoom in on things that might show it was fake. Our best bet is going to be if I can find the video's digital fingerprint through block chain technology. That fingerprint can help us show the video is fake. But it's going to take time."

"I'm back in court on Tuesday. And I'm not going to show."

"Didn't James vouch for you?"

I ignored this.

"What are my options? Besides finding the killer myself?"

Danny was silent for a second.

"I don't think this video would hold up in court."

"That's it?" I said. "My future depends on that: '*I don't think*?'"

"I'm pretty sure I can prove it's a fake. Then there is no case, right?"

"I can't wait for that. I'll be in touch soon," I said and hung up.

36

The van was what I liked to call a Kidnapper Van. In other words, it had no windows in the back. The only windows were the front windshield and the windows on the driver's side and passenger side.

Tony knew what I needed. There was a curtain you could pull that was right behind the seats so you had complete privacy in the back of the van.

Although the outside of the van was beat-up—dented with patches of bondo—the inside wasn't as bad. It was equipped as a temporary mobile home:

A thin twin mattress was on the floor with a military-style sleeping bag neatly rolled on top of it. There was something that I could only describe as a chamber pot with a screwed-on lid. Gross. But maybe necessary. Gallon-sized water bottles lined one wall, held back with a webbed strap. A milk crate held military rations. But the best part was the laptop. It was inside a case that looked like it would survive a drop from a twenty-story building. An index card taped to the top of it gave the log-in information and explained how to connect to a satellite Wi-Fi network. Sweet. A small box held two more burner phones that had not yet been activated. A duffel bag held some changes of clothing—thick woolen shirts, socks, and sweaters. A heavy wool pea coat lay on the bed too.

I had no idea how Tony pulled it all together so quickly but suspected this was all part of his own bug-out kit.

It was nearly dawn and I still hadn't slept. I was exhausted. I unrolled the sleeping bag and then leaned up against one cold wall of the van, pulling the laptop on my lap.

I logged in and started digging around, looking for information on Deepfake. But then I realized it was a waste of my time. Danny was handling that. I needed more info on our suspects. Right now, every person who was at that first gala fundraising meeting was a suspect. Someone there had targeted me that night.

I went down the list of names. For each name, I logged into search engines that only existed on the Dark Web.

After I researched the first five names, I didn't feel like I was any further along than when I'd started. One guy who had made his billions on a Silicon Valley start-up had a little bit of a sketchy background. He was dishonorably discharged from the military about fifteen years before for an incident involving "friendly fire." After digging deeper, I found that he'd lost his shit and accidentally shot up a home with women and children in Afghanistan. When one of his fellow soldiers had stumbled on the scene and tried to intervene, he'd turned and "accidentally" killed the man. *Holy fuck.* He could be the guy.

The entire thing had been covered up in the interest of "national security," allowing him to go on with his normal life. And apparently become a billionaire. What a joke. This guy was clearly unstable. I thought back, trying to remember any interactions I had with him. The only impression I had was that he was super arrogant, quiet, and talked to my chest instead of my face. Ew.

He was my best suspect so far. But what was his motivation? Maybe he was just a nutjob? But the murders were too methodical to be crimes of passion. There had to be a motivation. What would someone gain by killing members of the gala fundraising committee? Was he Jewish and offended by the opera like so many others? Maybe he was killing in protest?

I still needed to make my way down the list. I yawned and stretched. I wish I had a coffee maker in the van. Outside, I could hear the low murmur of voices. I got up to stretch more and peeked out the curtain. I could see a few fires in trash cans. It was just starting to get light. Dark figures huddled around them, and smoke poured out of them in plumes. I had a chill all the way down to my bones. I'd finish up and crawl into the sleeping bag. It would keep me warm. It was made for extreme cold.

Back on the bed, I decided to search Nicoletta Marchese.

After I waded through all the press clippings about her illustrious career, I had to admit I felt a bit jealous. She was a really accomplished opera singer. It explained a little bit about why she was such a diva. In fact, looking at the press on her, I was surprised she wasn't even more of a bitch. People adored her. She was sweet and attentive to her fans. She gave extravagantly to charity, and she'd had her heart broken two years ago by another opera singer she was engaged to. He ran off with a Brazilian model a decade younger. The press had covered the break-up ad nauseam, painting her as a sweet woman who had been wronged.

It made me question whether I was right to disapprove of her relationship with James. Maybe she really cared about him. Maybe she was really looking for love and had found it with him. I frowned. I just didn't buy it. As much as I wanted to believe that she might be good for James, something stopped me. It was gut instinct. I listened to that. I'd learned over the years that ignoring it was only at my own peril.

I decided to dig deeper.

I used some Dark Web tricks to dig up photos from her childhood, teen, and young adult years. Some were on her mother's Facebook page.

Yawning, I idly scrolled through pictures of her as a young girl and then into ones of her as a teen. Then I froze.

She was at a high school dance with a young man who looked familiar. I zoomed in on the picture. It looked like Charles Wellington. Then I scrolled through the "likes" and the comments and found someone with the same last name. It was a woman.

I clicked on that profile.

The account was disabled, but as I'd learned, once something was online, it would never truly disappear. I accessed the old account and realized it was Charles's mother's. She had died four years earlier. She had tons of pictures of him as an opera singer. And she had pictures of Nicoletta and Charles together all through high school.

So, Nicoletta and Charles were high school sweethearts.

Then I saw something that made me sit up straighter.

Four years ago. Right before the woman died. A picture of Charles and Nicoletta on a beach in a tropical location. The woman had written: My greatest wish is for these two to finally marry and make me a grandma. I now realize I won't be around for it, but they have both promised to make this a reality so I can finally die in peace."

I leaned back against the van wall. Holy fuck.

There was so much to take in about this revelation.

Charles and Nicoletta.

Were a thing. But Charles had been with Oliver Hollingsworth.

And he and Nicoletta seemed just fine.

Sure, there was a chance they'd parted ways amicably, and Nicoletta gave her blessing to his relationship with Oliver, but I somehow doubted it. If Charles had recently come out of the closet, would he be with Oliver or some other hot young guy? Maybe. I just didn't know.

It seemed more likely that Charles was fucking Oliver for his money.

I decided the first thing to do after I took a nap would be to do some reconnaissance on Charles and Nicoletta.

I crawled into the sleeping bag and closed my eyes. When I opened them again the sun was setting. Shit. So much for a quick nap.

I dug through the duffel bag that Tony had left in the corner. I pulled on a thick, military-style wool turtleneck, a thick wool pea coat, and black stocking cap. I pulled these on, tucking my hair inside the hat and pulling the jacket collar up around my neck.

I was pretty sure I looked like a dude. Perfect. Then I got behind the wheel and started the van, grateful as heat began to pour out the vents. I'd stop and get a huge cup of coffee at an out-of-the-way gas station and then head to the address I'd found for Nicoletta.

37

The gas station clerk probably thought I was going to rob him when I walked in, because between the black stocking cap, big sunglasses, and my coat collar pulled up to my cheekbones, I was obviously trying to disguise my face.

But I didn't want any cameras to be able to identify me.

If someone had the tech savvy to create a Deepfake video of me, who knows if they were able to tap into facial recognition software on the underground network of cameras filming through the city.

Armed with a large coffee and some snacks, I headed toward Nicoletta's place in the Richmond District for my stakeout. It was now dark. There was a chance it would be a bust. She might have turned in for the night, and I'd stare at her house as she slept peacefully through the night. That was okay. I had to do something. I would go crazy if I didn't at least feel like I was trying to figure it all out.

I parked across the street from the apartment building and then approached the door. Nobody was around. I scanned the names on the doorbells. N. Marchese. Bingo. But it didn't say what floor or apartment number. This might be more of a fool's errand than I realized.

After I crossed the street and was about to get back in the van, I scanned the bank of windows facing the street. Then I walked further down to look at the side of the building. It appeared the apartments ran the length of the building from front to back. As I was standing there, a cab pulled up in front of the building. I shrank into the shadows.

It was a young man who stumbled out of the cab and loudly thanked the driver. Then he was inside, and the street was quiet again.

Back in the van, I took a chance and kept it running to keep the heat on. A thick bank of fog had rolled in and hovered just above the street lights, making the temperature drop dramatically. Even with the pea coat and heater on, I was cold.

I was yawning and sipping the last dregs of my coffee when another car pulled up.

A strawberry blonde wearing a fur coat stepped out.

Nicoletta.

Quickly, she stepped inside the front door.

I got out of the van so I could see which apartment window lit up.

Light turned in a window on the second floor. I could see Nicoletta shed her coat and lean over a small table.

I was about to cross the street when I noticed the car that had dropped her off was slowly rolling down the street. *Fuck.*

As I ducked behind the van, the car, a small black sedan, parked.

The driver got out.

Charles.

Perfect.

I watched as he walked over to the front door and let himself in with a key. I waited a beat and then quickly crossed the street.

I used a credit card to pop the front door and raced up the stairs to the second floor. The second-floor hallway split the building in half. There was a door on the right and one on the left. Nicoletta's apartment was the one on the left, so I headed toward that door as quietly as I could. The building was ancient and the wooden floors in the hall creaked loudly as I walked.

I took my time, though, and soon had my ear pressed against the door. I could only hear some sultry music—Massive Attack or something. I waited for about ten minutes and finally gave up. Outside, I looked up at her window. It was dark. Lights out.

Back in the van, I tried to stay awake, keeping my eyes on the front door. It wasn't until just before dawn that the door opened and Charles slipped out. I waited until his sedan passed me and then pulled out about a block behind him. I followed him until we got to Pacific Heights with all the multi-millionaire dollar mansions. I kept driving down the street as he pulled into the underground garage of a massive home.

I'd bet my last dollar it was Oliver Hollingsworth's house.

Looks like Charles was, at the very least, a very naughty boy. At the most, he might be a stone-cold killer.

I dialed Tony on one of the burner phones.

"Yo."

"How tough would it be to get a nanny cam? I need to stick it in this opera singer's apartment. I think she's involved with these murders."

"Give me the address. It's handled."

"She's home now," I protested. "I'll go stake her out and then get inside the apartment when she leaves. If you could just buy the nanny cam for me so I'm not on the CCTV cameras—."

"Address. I got this," he said, cutting me off.

"But I—."

"Santella. I said I got this. Give me the address."

Feeling like a little kid, I obeyed and reeled it off.

"Thanks," I said and hung up, feeling like I was going to cry.

After so many years of always doing things on my own, it always threw me for a loop when people like Tony stepped in to help. I wasn't used to people taking care of me.

There had been a few years with Nico when I'd been able to relax and be taken care of, but for the vast majority of my life, I'd been on my own.

It was hard to accept, but right then, I needed to swallow my pride or stubbornness or stupidness or whatever it was, and accept help. I was in over my head.

38

Charles woke Oliver by sticking his face in the old man's junk.

Soon, the geezer was clutching at Charles for dear life.

Then Charles flipped the bony body over and stuck it in, pumping away furiously.

After a night with Nicoletta, Charles was proud he could come again so easily.

Luckily, Oliver liked it a little rough. Charles felt as if his revulsion and hatred were barely disguised, but the old guy ate it up. He'd once told Charles that he'd been initiated into the gay world by his opera teacher, who thought sex went hand in hand with physical abuse.

Charles didn't play that way, but he had slapped the old guy once or twice during sex when Oliver begged for it.

He figured that if the old man had woken in the night and realized he wasn't in bed, being awoken in this manner would quash any questions or doubts.

Charles was counting the fucking hours until he never had to fuck an old bag of bones again.

Thinking of the millions he was going to inherit made it oh, so much easier. He'd have done a lot worse for money. In fact, as an older teen, he'd done worse—much worse. The things he'd done to other teenage boys now made him sick to his stomach. He blocked most of it out of his memory. He'd done what it took to survive on the streets at the time.

His father had kicked him out after catching him fucking the neighbor boy.

He'd tried to explain that he wasn't actually gay, that he was going to marry Nicoletta. That the boy was paying him a hundred dollars to suck him off. And that he was going to use the money to take Nicoletta to prom since his father was a cheap fucking alcoholic who wouldn't part with a dime. But his father hadn't bothered to listen to any of that.

So in essence, it was his father who made him bisexual. He'd turned what was going to be a one-time thing into a way for Charles to survive.

After Oliver went down to eat his breakfast of a hard-boiled egg and toast, Charles hopped in the shower.

Only then did he allow himself to ruminate over his new problem.

He wasn't an idiot.

He knew that a van had followed him home from Nicoletta's place.

It had done a damn good job of trailing him. If he hadn't been paying attention, he would have missed it.

It was a problem.

Somebody knew about him and Nicoletta.

If it was Gia Santella, it didn't really matter. She'd been arrested for the murders so far. As far as he was concerned, it was a done deal. There was only one last step to take.

He was waiting for Marshall to give him the okay that the

video was ready. Now that she was out on bail, it would have to be tonight.

It was important that he and Nicoletta have a rock-solid alibi for this last murder. If they were at rehearsal with dozens of others, they could not possibly be connected to Oliver's murder. The Deepfake footage would show Gia committing the murder. Two nights ago, they'd taken the first steps with Nicoletta standing in again for Gia. Oliver had been out at the time, so Charles had laid in bed pretending to be Oliver while the security cameras in Oliver's house filmed the whole thing. The footage showed Nicoletta coming in the unlocked back door and then going into Oliver's bedroom. There, she'd placed a pillow over his face. Marshall had said it would be simple to place Oliver's face on his own in the final footage. Then Nicoletta leaned over and placed the gun square on the pillow. Marshall had said he would be able to grab the actual murder footage from there, showing the gun firing.

Marshall had already tapped into Oliver's security system. By the time Charles came home and reported finding Oliver dead, the security footage would be replaced with the Deepfake video.

It was foolproof. It was brilliant.

Once the will was executed, Charles would pay off Marshall and then disappear. Without him, the opera would be canceled. He would arrange it to look like he'd been murdered by a crazy person protesting the opera. A week or so later, Nicoletta would follow him, saying she had been ordered by her doctor to take a hiatus after the harassment she'd suffered during the rehearsals.

The only possible thing that could stand in his way was whoever was in that old van.

But he wouldn't worry about it now.

As he washed the soap off his body, he stretched. He felt great.

Being with Nicoletta almost all night had energized him. He couldn't wait until they could be together forever.

If he was really lucky, this morning's sex was the last time he'd have to stick it in the old fucker.

By this time tomorrow, he'd be planning a funeral.

39

PARKED BACK IN THE HOMELESS CAMP UNDER THE OVERPASS, I put the van's alarm on and crawled into the back, ready to nap for as long as I could. I felt safer sleeping during the day anyway. Anyone who tried to break into the van would be doing it in front of everyone in the homeless camp. Plus, by the time I'd pulled up, most of the people had already cleared out, going to beg or get food or whatever it was they did during their days.

By the time I woke up, it was late afternoon, and I knew James was freaking the fuck out.

I grabbed a burner phone and dialed.

"It's me."

"Where are you?" He sounded pissed.

"I'm safe. I think I know who the killer is."

"Gia, I'm not fucking around. You need to turn yourself in immediately."

"I can't."

"My entire life, my career, my reputation, my future, is on the fucking line."

Yeah. He was ticked off.

"You're going to have to trust me here, James." Even as I said the words, doubt filled me, and my stomach clenched. If I blew this, not only was my life destroyed, but his would be as well.

"Gia, turn yourself in and we'll figure the rest out."

"I'm sorry, I can't do that."

I hung up and felt sick.

I logged onto my laptop and started digging around.

There were a lot of Deepfake videos.

Maybe proving my case wouldn't be that hard after all.

A notification popped up suddenly. I stared at it.

It was a notification that movement had been detected on an external camera. I looked around the van for a second. Did the van have surveillance cameras I hadn't known about? That Tony was magical. I clicked on the icon and then sat back in surprise.

It was the nanny cam in Nicoletta's apartment, and it was filming her fucking Charles.

Holy shit!

I saw her mouth moving, but there was no sound. I fiddled around until I found the volume control.

"Oh, baby. You fuck me so good."

Boring. Think of something more original, dumbass. But I hit record.

Obviously when this was all over, James would have to learn the truth about his dear, sweet girlfriend.

I opened up a can of beans and ate them with a spoon while I waited for Lover Boy to shoot his load. Finally, he did, thank God. I was sick of watching his skinny ass pump away to the chanteuse's breathy moans.

He stood up and walked naked across the room, his member still at attention. He poured a drink and then sat in an armchair with his legs spread.

"Cover your junk at least!" I said to the empty van.

"Charlie," the songbird simpered. "When can we leave? When are we gonna off the old guy?"

He gave a slow smile and crooked his finger. She willingly came over before him.

"Tonight, angel. He's a dead man before morning."

"Oh, goodie," she said and clapped her hands together like a five-year-old.

She made me sick. For so many reasons.

"I'm heading out in a few minutes to make his drink for cocktail hour. I'll put some sleeping pills in the drink, but it won't come up during the autopsy. I made a point to tell his doctor last visit that I was worried he drinks and takes sleeping pills at the same time. It's documented."

"Oh, you're so smart honey," she said.

"The cameras are all set up. Marshall has the whole thing rigged. The time stamp on the cameras in the mansion will show the murder at the exact same time we are at the opera house doing rehearsals."

"Brilliant!" she said and took his drink from him. She sipped at it and then licked her lips. "Did you already see the video? Did I do good?"

"You deserve an Oscar, baby. All the way."

"When can we leave town?" she said and pouted. "I hate it here."

"I'm not sure how long it will take to execute the will, but the second the money clears my account, we're out of here."

"I love you so much!" she said, pulling a sweater on over her bare breasts and tugging on some leggings and boots.

"Let's go," he said. "You can wait in the car. It shouldn't take more than a half hour, and then we'll head straight to rehearsal."

He quickly dressed and they were out the door.

Fuck.

I stopped the recording.

They were going to go kill Oliver Kingsley Hollingsworth. Tonight.

I had to stop them.

I grabbed another burner phone and dialed James's cell phone.

It went straight to voice mail. *Motherfucker.*

I left a message: "I'm going to Oliver Hollingsworth's house. Charles is headed there to kill him. He's the murderer. And I'm sorry to tell you this, but Nicoletta is his accomplice. I'll explain it all soon, but you need to get someone over there to stop the murder."

I hung up and dialed 911.

"911. What is your emergency?"

"There's about to be a murder. Someone is going to kill Oliver Kingsley Hollingsworth. Please send squads to his house."

"What is your name?"

"We don't have time for this," I said, jumping into the van's driver's seat.

"What is the address?"

"Fuck. I don't know. Look it up. He's a rich old dude who basically is the San Francisco Opera."

"Ma'am, we can't do anything without an address."

I hung up and dialed Danny.

He gave me Hollingsworth's address practically before I finished saying 'Hollingsworth.'

"I don't know how to get there," I moaned.

"Where are you now?"

I told him.

"It's going to take you at least fifteen minutes," Danny said. "Turn right on the Embarcadero. Otherwise, you're going to end up in traffic and on dead-end streets. I'll have you go the long way around."

"I don't have time for the long way?"

"Trust me, it will be the short way."

"How long will it take Charles from the Richmond District?"

"Five minutes."

"Motherfuck."

"I'll send you the address to plug into your phone."

"It's a burner. I don't even have GPS or anything."

"Okay. I'll walk you through it."

I grabbed another phone and dialed 911 again.

"There's about to be a murder at this address," I said and reeled off the address.

"What's your name?"

"I can't tell you."

"What number are you calling from?"

"I can't tell you."

"We are going to need more information?"

"You fucking kidding me? I just said someone is about to die at that address. Even if you think I'm a nut job, could you at least do me a favor and have someone call or check on Mr. Hollingsworth. Do one of those...what do you call it? Welfare checks. Yes. Do a welfare check on him. Please!"

Meanwhile, Danny was yelling in my ear. "Turn right on Union. No...left. Shit. Keep going and then make your next left."

I wanted to scream.

I called 911 again on the other phone, and this time it was busy.

"What is wrong with a city, if it's 911 line is busy? I'm calling the mayor," I shouted to nobody.

"Turn right."

I had nearly gone past the street, so I yanked the steering wheel, and the tires laid rubber down and squealed. An older man gave me a dirty look.

Oops.

"Turn left."

It was the street.

"I'm close."

"Can you find it now?" Danny asked.

I looked at the addresses. "Yes. It's on this block."

I slowed down. Then I saw Charles's car. It was parked in front of a very large four-story house, towering over the other very large houses in the neighborhood.

There was a familiar redhead in the passenger seat.

I parked right behind her, grabbing James's gun and racing toward the door without bothering to close the door to the van. As I passed, I caught a glimpse of her face as she saw me, and her mouth opened into a wide O.

I was worried I was too late.

40

THE FRONT DOOR WAS LOCKED. I DIDN'T HAVE TIME TO FUCK around with picking the lock, so I fired my gun and blew it right off the door. I didn't care about drawing attention to myself. In fact, I was hoping the neighbors would call the cops.

I raced inside and then stopped. I had no idea where to go. There was an elevator to my right. That's when I saw it was on the third floor. I assumed that's where the bedrooms were. Beside the elevator was a set of stairs. I raced up the stairs, keeping the gun in front of me. At the top of the landing for the third floor, I paused, heart racing. I heard the sound of a floor creaking down the hall, so I swiftly headed that way, keeping my back to the wall.

Even though it wasn't dark outside yet, the third floor was dim. Heavy, light-blocking drapes covered all the windows. As I came to each door, I quickly looked inside. There were bedrooms and sitting rooms and even two libraries. I heard another sound. A low murmur. It was coming from the end of the hall. Then I heard a clear voice say, "Let's get you tucked in."

Charles.

I raced to the end of the hall.

I stepped into the doorway in time to see Charles place a pillow over Hollingsworth's face. He was holding it with one hand. His other hand was clutching a handgun. I could see Hollingsworth's feet under the covers at the foot of the bed, kicking.

"Stop!" I shouted and pointed my gun at Charles.

But it's too late. I watched in horror as the pillow exploded in a pink puff of blood and feathers.

My finger was about to squeeze off a round when I hear a low familiar voice behind me.

"Drop the gun."

It's Nicoletta.

I whirled. She was holding a small handgun. It's pointed at my forehead.

I felt another gun in the small of my back.

I crouched and gently set my gun on the floor.

"Stay down," Charles said, drawing back a few feet but keeping the gun pointed at me.

"Fuck you." I scrambled on all fours to the corner. I wanted something solid behind my back. I'm frantically thinking of how to get out of this situation.

Nicoletta tucked her gun back into a small handbag. But then didn't move. She stood and stared at me.

"What are you going to do with her?" she said.

"Get back in the car. Now. You can't be here. I don't want them to think you're involved."

"Don't worry, baby," she says. "I just called James and told him that Gia Santella told me she was going to kill herself by jumping off the Golden Gate bridge. They all went there instead. We have a few minutes."

"You're so smart," Charles said. "I need to clean up a few things around here so go wait in the car. Okay?"

She hesitated. "What about her?"

She was looking at me.

"I'll take care of her. I've got a plan. She's going to do exactly what you said, 'Kill herself.' But she's going to do it right here. Remorse and all that."

"Oh good."

"Go on, now," he said. "This isn't something you want to see."

Nicoletta hesitated and then I heard her heels click-clacking down the hall.

Charles waited a beat and then reached over and shoved the end of his gun into my mouth. I gagged and tasted metal.

Then he grabbed the neck of my shirt, ripping it down to my waist and started to tug down my pants.

When I tried to fight back, he withdrew the gun and in one smooth motion pistol whipped me. For a second I saw stars and realized I was now flat on my back on the wooden floor. Meanwhile, Charles was above me, straddling my chest, mumbling obscenities.

He talked about wanting to fuck me since the first time he saw me and a bunch of other bullshit. I glared up at him and tried to spit in his face, but it just dripped down the side of my mouth.

"Fuck you!" I screamed and tried to push up. He had me pinned. He was sitting on my chest. I could barely breathe. He held my hands pinned above my head with one arm and then with his other, he reached down to undo his pants.

I brought a knee up sharply and managed to graze his groin. He groaned and briefly released my hands to lift my head by the hair and slam my head into the floor again. When he reached back up to pin my hands, I managed to get one hand free.

He was fumbling with his pants and then reaching for my thighs, trying to part my legs, when I heard a soft sound.

It was Nicoletta. She was standing behind him in bare feet,

holding her heeled sandals in her hand. Her face was expressionless. She held a finger up to her lips.

I met her eyes. She gave me a slight nod.

Charles managed to part my legs. His head was facing down as he let go of my hand and used both of his hands to try to maneuver his dick into the right place. I didn't fight back because right then Nicoletta walked over to the gun and crouched down. Using her handbag, she knocked the gun toward me. It skidded across the floor and came to rest by my free hand.

Before Charles could react, I had the gun in my hand and shoved under his chin.

His eyes widened in surprise but then went blank as I pulled the trigger.

I scrambled out from under the dead weight of his body, trying to wipe blood and bone off my face. As soon as my ears stopped ringing I heard shouting. I looked around. The room was empty. Nicoletta was gone.

I was pushing bloody sticky strands of hair back from my face when the police rushed in. Instead of helping me, they threw me on the floor and snapped handcuffs on me.

41

As soon as the district attorney saw the video I recorded, I was released from jail.

Dante picked me up.

"Jesus, Gia," he said as he looked me over.

I was still covered in blood and bone. They threw a towel at me, but it hadn't done much good dry.

I looked around the lobby as I followed Dante to the parking lot.

No James.

"I need to call James," I said as soon as I got into Dante's car.

"He's not taking any of this very well."

"He's not?" I shouted in astonishment. "*He's* not taking this well? How about me being a murder suspect and him not even believing I was innocent and me about to go away on a murder rap. And he's not taking this well? Well, fuck."

Dante explained that James had found out Nicoletta had used him for months. And she wasn't pregnant. He'd gone to see her after my arrest, and she'd coldly told him she'd never been pregnant and never cared about him.

"He didn't believe me. He believed her. I was almost raped and killed because he took her word over mine."

"Is she in custody?"

"She's cooperating with police," Dante said. "She claims that Charles was threatening her. He told her if she went to the police about his plans, he'd kill her, too. She has a boatload of evidence proving Charles killed all those people. Apparently, he wanted the police to think that Hollingsworth's murder was just one of a string of murders committed because of the controversial opera."

"Why did he make me the scape goat then?"

Dante shrugged.

"Dante, they were fucking. I heard them. They were making plans to be together after they murdered Oliver Hollingsworth."

"She was playing him then. Police found a one-way ticket in her name to Vienna, Austria."

"So she was fucking him over, too. She was fucking him and James over. Literally and figuratively."

"I think so."

"I'm fucking furious with James," I said. "How could he have been so stupid?"

"Gia," Dante said calmly. "That's why he's so fucked up. Think about how guilty he feels about that? He's taken a leave of absence. He said he had to get his head together. He didn't believe you and you almost paid the price with your life."

Dante was right. I was pissed. I glared out the window at the people walking on the sidewalk.

"In the end, it was Nicoletta who was responsible for the charges being dropped even if she didn't realize it," Dante said. "In her hurry to throw Charles under the bus, she basically proved that you didn't do anything. She's also helping them convict the guy who did the Deepfake video. He lives in Switzerland or something, so it could be tough to get him extradited."

"What a cluster fuck," I said as a BMW cut us off and Dante laid on the horn. "I just want to go home and take a shower and then sleep for the next year."

"Home?" Dante said. "You think of the hotel as home now?"

He sounded so excited I didn't have the heart to say something snarky.

"Yeah," I said. "I think it will be home at least for a while."

"Great!" he said. "Because we sign papers this week!"

"The old guy agreed even though we didn't find out who was embezzling."

"You did find out, actually. It was Maxwell. He knew Herr Janson was going to sell in a few years, and he wanted to buy it. He's worked here since he was fourteen."

"Idiot."

"Dead idiot," Dante said as he pulled into the circular drive at the hotel.

Up in my suite, Dante waited in the living room while I took a long shower and changed into a pair of baggy sweatpants and a soft T-shirt.

When I came out, he had a plate of hot pasta waiting for me.

"Remember I used to make this for you when you were sick, when we were teenagers and you were hung over?" he asked. "I snuck up to the restaurant and made it."

"You're sneaky. And fast," I said and took a big bite.

"And talented?"

"True." I smiled. "You're the only one who has always been there for me."

"We're *famiglia*, Gia."

I took another big bite of the garlicky, buttery pasta.

It was perfect.

Shortly after cleaning my plate, I crawled in bed and slept for fourteen hours.

The next day my phone rang. It was James.

"I'm sorry. I'm sorry I didn't believe you."

"I forgive you," I said. I didn't make a big deal of it. I knew that apology cost him dearly. In many ways.

"I'm leaving town."

"I heard."

We were both silent for a few seconds.

"It's not your fault," I finally said. "She was a really good con artist."

He didn't respond.

"Where you going?" I asked.

"Serbia," he said.

"Really?" I was flabbergasted.

"Yes. You have a problem with that?"

I frowned. I didn't like his dickish attitude. I knew he was hiding his hurt, but it still sucked.

"Take care of yourself. I'll miss you," I said.

He didn't answer, just hung up.

I wasn't too worried about it. He'd get over it. We'd had heated arguments and conversations before. It was no big deal. We'd be fine the next time we spoke or saw each other. At least that was what I was telling myself. I just hoped he wouldn't spend too much time beating himself up over that stupid opera bitch.

A few days after I spoke to James, I was busy making arrangements for the construction crews to work on the hotel. The deal had finalized earlier that week, and Dante and I had celebrated with a private champagne dinner at the restaurant.

We'd decided to redo the hotel one floor at a time, so we could keep it operational during reconstruction.

I was hunched over the paperwork and blueprints when the phone in my room rang. I yawned and picked it up. Usually, the only people who called on it were hotel staff or room service.

"'lo?" I said.

"Is this Gia Santella?"

The voice was familiar.

"Yes, this is she."

"This is Anthony Ferraro."

The mayor.

"I tried your other number…"

"I lost that phone."

"Oh," he said.

"That's fine, Mayor," I said formally. "What can I do for you?"

I knew he had agreed to speak to the planning commission about the permits and the street closures. But Dante had been the one dealing with him on those issues.

"I have two tickets to a moonlight cruise on the bay and was hoping you would come with me. It's supposed to be a full moon, and the weather is spectacular."

I looked toward the window. I'd been at my desk in my hotel room all day, but it did look wonderful outside.

My first instinct was to say no. I had too much work to do. Because I took so long to answer, he must've sensed my hesitation.

"I know you're really busy," he said. "Dante told me that you've been locked up in that hotel room for three days. That's one reason I decided to buy the tickets. I'm trying to save you from yourself. You need a break. I'm the same as you, Gia. I tend to work too hard. But trust me when I say a tiny break will be good, and you'll be able to get after everything with a fresh start in the morning."

It was a convincing speech. I was smiling by the time he was done.

"No wonder you were elected mayor," I said.

He laughed loud and long. A real, genuine, hearty laugh that made me laugh too.

"So, is that a yes?"

"You win. What time? And what's the dress code?"

"I'll be there to pick you up at seven, and the dress code—let's just say it's cocktail attire."

"See you then," I said softly and hung up.

My attention was back on my laptop. I spent the rest of the afternoon putting together a final cost analysis for my company—they had agreed to finance the remodeling but needed estimates and hard quotes from every contractor and subcontractor involved. I'd just finished a draft of the document when there was a knock on the hotel room door.

It was only then that I noticed the sun was setting. I glanced at the clock. Seven. The mayor was at the door.

Shit.

I raced to the door and flung it open. He stood there in a black button-down shirt and black pants, and he looked like Clark Kent come to call.

"I'm so sorry," I said. "I lost track of time. The cost analysis for the remodeling is due in the morning."

He just stood there in the doorway, grinning, until I finished speaking.

"You going to wear that?"

I looked down at my outfit. I was in bare feet, running shorts and an oversized sweatshirt falling off one shoulder. I had no makeup on, and my dark hair was piled on my head in a messy bun.

"No. Shit. Make yourself a drink," I said, flustered. I was already racing toward the bedroom. "I'll only be a second."

In my room, I stepped under the fastest shower of all time, and when I got out, I slipped on a knee-length little black dress. I sprayed perfume, slicked on some red lipstick and shook out my hair from its bun. Then I grabbed my Jimmy Choo stilettos and my bag and raced to to the living room. He was standing at the window looking out at the Golden Gate.

"Are we late?"

He turned, and his eyes raked over me. I suddenly felt self-conscious.

"That's the fastest I've ever seen a woman get ready in my life," he said and gave me a slow smile. I was about to make an excuse when he spoke more. "And yet, I'm not sure anyone has ever looked so good."

I sat there with my mouth open. I was used to charming men, but he took the cake. I could feel my cheeks get hot, so I turned away and slipped on my heels, heading for the door.

"I'm ready if you are."

He was instantly beside me.

"I'm sorry, I should've told you to take your time," he said in a low voice near my neck. "I didn't want you to rush."

"I don't want us to miss the cruise," I said.

That's when he reached out and brushed a stray lock of hair out of my eyes.

"Didn't I tell you it's a private cruise?"

I shook my head. "Uh, no."

"We can get there any time."

"I'm ready," I said. For some reason, he unnerved me. It was so strange. He made me feel unsettled. And out of control. Most men didn't have that effect on me. Usually I was the one calling the shots. I wasn't sure if I liked it or hated it.

He put his hand on the small of my back as we made our way to the elevator, and I fought the feeling to turn around and jump him. He was so hot. And so...dangerous.

I knew before I even stepped into the elevator that I'd made a huge mistake agreeing to see him again.

Four hours later, I knew I'd been right.

I should've stayed far, far away from this man.

We were barely able to keep our hands off each other all night. His touch was electrifying.

By the time we stepped into the elevator in the hotel lobby, we were all over each other. He had my dress down to my waist, and I had unbuttoned his shirt.

"Every time I've seen you, you've been in a fancy dress, but I can honestly say you have never looked so sexy as you did standing there in shorts with your hair up and no makeup."

"Knock it off, Ferraro. You know you're already getting laid, you don't have to charm me anymore," I said.

"I'm telling the truth." Then he kissed my neck and I melted.

"Okay, I believe you."

Thank God the elevator opened up to my private hallway, because I was half naked and panting.

We were still making out as we stumbled toward the door to my suite. I managed to flick the key card and then we were inside.

"Bedroom," I growled.

He lifted me up to carry me to the bedroom, and I had wrapped both of my legs around his waist when a familiar voice rang out from the living room.

"Maybe I should have called first."

Ryder.

Things just got complicated.

The story continues in *Deadly Justice*, the next Gia Santella Thriller. Head to the next page for a sneak peek or order today by clicking the link or scanning the QR code below!
www.amazon.com/B08VRF3GNT

Stay up to date with Kristi Belcamino's new releases by clicking the link or scanning the QR code below!
https://liquidmind.media/kristi-belcamino-newsletter-signup-1-first-vengeance/
(You'll receive a **free** copy of *First Vengeance: A Gia Santella Prequel!*)

Did you enjoy *Dark Justice*? Click the link or scan the QR code below to let us know your thoughts!
www.amazon.com/B08P7RHQJ5

Dark Justice

DEADLY JUSTICE CHAPTER ONE

A week before

"Well, this is awkward."

Mayor Anthony Ferraro was a master at understatement.

It was my second date with the mayor of San Francisco. Only because he was so damn persistent. I'd tried to blow him off. For starters, he was Italian. I mean, I was Italian-American, too, but that didn't mean I thought it was a good idea to date another Italian. He was handsome with gorgeous olive skin but looked like he spent his spare time getting mani-pedis. He was just a little "too" pretty and groomed, as if his fancy suits could stand up on their own.

We Italians called men like this, "mammones." They were mama's boys who lived at home, sponging off mama's cooking and cleaning until they were in their forties. Like I said, an Italian man. Better off to avoid them all. They were either mammones or macho pricks.

I liked my men a little more rugged and independent. Like ... Ryder.

Despite this, I agreed to go on a moonlight bay cruise with

the mayor and was almost pissed to discover that I was actually attracted to him. He was confident, witty, and powerful–qualities I found incredibly sexy and alluring.

So much so that I was eager to get back to my hotel suite and get his pants off.

After a hot and heavy elevator ride up to my hotel suite, we stumbled through the door in a mad embrace only to hear Ryder's voice interrupting us.

I rarely grew flustered, but I could feel my face grow warm.

It got worse as I looked around. The suite was lit with dozens of candles. The sultry sounds of Etta James filled the air.

And then I got a good look at Ryder.

Good god. The man was only wearing a white hotel towel wrapped around his waist.

His hair was longer now, wet and slicked back. A droplet of water still gleamed on his tanned and sleek chest. His tattooed arms rippled with muscles.

For once I was speechless.

The mayor, however, was not.

"I'm guessing it's safe to assume you know this man and he's not a burglar who broke into your room?"

I was snapped out of my silence.

"I do know him. He's not a burglar, but he definitely did break into my room."

"Don't get me wrong," the mayor said, looking at Ryder. "You're a good-looking guy and all, but I'm not really into threesomes. Maybe you should go."

I side eyed the mayor. I'd never seen this side of him—semi-bossy alpha male.

I was debating whether to toss them both out and let them have it out in the hall when Ryder spoke.

"Entirely my fault, bro," Ryder said. "I should've called first."

Bro?

"Do you have a place to stay?" I asked Ryder, ignoring the mayor and his macho posturing.

Ryder didn't live in the states. He lived in the south of France, which made his appearance in my hotel room even more surreal.

Ryder responded by dropping the towel. He was naked. He was quite a specimen—which I already knew, of course.

I saw the mayor's eyes narrow. "I see," he said and raised his eyebrow slightly.

Ryder just winked as he reached for a pile of clothes.

"Oh, stop it," I said. "You two are acting like teenage boys."

I was surprised the mayor didn't whip his cock out to compare.

Ryder tugged on a pair of jeans, sans underwear.

"I can find a place to stay," he said as he pulled on a tight black tee-shirt. "If that's what you really want."

I frowned and bit my lip. I had no idea what I really wanted.

"I think I'm going to call it a night," Anthony said and reached for the door. Then he was gone. I looked around frantically. Fuck.

"Ryder. Stay put. I'll be right back."

I caught up with Anthony right when he punched the down button on the elevator.

"I don't know what to say," I said.

"Well, clearly."

Again, I wasn't sure whether to be impressed by his wit or furious.

"Listen, Ryder lives in France. He's *supposed* to be halfway across the world. I had no idea he was here. I had no idea he was *coming* here. I have no idea how he got into my room, but that's another issue."

The mayor scoffed as the elevator door opened and he stepped inside. I followed him part way.

"Listen. I like you," I said, taking his hands and looking up at him. "I had a different idea on how I wanted this night to end."

I was standing in the door of the elevator. He stuck out a foot on each side to keep the doors from closing.

He surprised me by smiling.

"I had all sorts of ideas. Some I think you might have really liked."

I smiled back.

"I understand if you don't want to see me again—if it's too complicated for you," I said. Because I'm going to be honest, this is nothing. My life is way more complicated in much worse ways than finding a naked guy in my hotel room."

He sighed. "Gia. I already know this. I know you and the life you live are as far from normal and ordinary as anyone I've ever met."

He was right. What else could I say? I opened my mouth to respond but he spoke first.

"That's why you are so damn intriguing. I don't want normal. I don't want ordinary. I want you."

Well, damn.

His eyes bore into me. I stood on tiptoe and looped my arms around his neck. He bowed his head and gave me a long, searing kiss. My body was pressed against his and the elevator doors whooshed shut behind us.

Finally, I drew back and hit the button to open the elevator doors again.

"I'll call you," I said, searching his eyes.

"Will you?"

I didn't answer. I just stood there and watched him as the elevator doors closed. I waited until I saw the elevator heading toward the first floor before I returned to the room.

Back in the room, Ryder was putting on his leather jacket.

"I think I should try this again," he said. "I'll go to the lobby and call you and yell 'surprise' and tell you I'm in town, downstairs actually, and you'll tell me tomorrow would be better and then we meet for breakfast.

I stared at him.

Fuck, he was hot.

He watched my eyes roam his body and a sly smile appeared on his face.

I shook my head no.

"Or," he said, shrugging out of his jacket, "we could just take it from here."

I was on him in two seconds, my mouth on his, my hands feverishly tugging off his jeans and untucking his shirt.

My body knew him so well. And wanted him.

I felt a slight shiver of guilt knowing that I'd just kissed the mayor but that fleeting thought disappeared as he lifted me up and I wrapped my legs around his waist. He swept a stack of books I had piled on the table to the floor and pressed me onto the table, my dress lifted up around my waist. I shut off my brain and let my body take over.

Sex with Ryder consumed me in ways that I both loved and hated at the same time.

I was a fool to think I'd be able to turn him away.

The only way to resist Ryder was to put an ocean or two between us.

Otherwise I was putty in his hands.

DEADLY JUSTICE CHAPTER TWO

Ryder and I rarely left my hotel suite for three days.

So what if the staff thought I was eccentric? After all, I owned the hotel now. Well, Dante and I did.

We ordered room service and I only left once or twice on hotel business.

One morning, I had an all-staff meeting to run and was gone for a few hours.

When I got back to the room, Ryder was hunched over a computer.

I came up behind him and kissed the back of his neck. He turned and wrapped his arms around me.

I glanced over his shoulder. My heart sank.

"You're leaving?"

He was looking at flights to France.

"I was commissioned for a job."

Ryder was ex-special forces. His current job was a mixture of security guard and part-time assassin.

He knew my history. I knew his—he was paid to take out people who I secretly hoped were evil. I couldn't stomach the thought of him killing innocents. Plus, it just didn't jive with who he was as a person. So I chose to believe he was "eradicating" scumbags.

"When do you have to leave?" I asked, hating the whining in my voice.

"I'm negotiating that right now."

He closed the laptop. Discussion over.

Knowing our time might be short made every moment with him even more poignant.

We talked late into the night, sharing childhood memories and darker, more haunting reminiscences of the evil we'd both encountered.

He allowed me to talk about the darker side of my life that I usually had to keep tucked deep inside. Even with Nico—who had been a cartel leader and ordered more deaths than I cared to even consider—I hadn't shared this much. Nico had men who did his dirty work. Unlike Nico, I had blood on my hands.

Ryder understood that.

Once, when Ryder was out on my deck smoking, Anthony called.

"Hi," I said, glancing at Ryder's back as he leaned over the rail, the Golden Gate glowing in the sunset beyond him.

"Let me know when we can finish what we started," he said.

I sighed.

"I know, I know," he said. "It's complicated." His voice was sarcastic but also playful.

"Ryder and I have history." It was a lame response. "Loose ends."

"Ryder is such a virile, studly, macho name," Anthony said. "Can't compete with that. But that's not why I called - Of course I want to see you again. Call me when you tie up those loose ends."

I hung up.

Three days later, Anthony called again.

Ryder hadn't mentioned the job back in France and I certainly hadn't brought it up.

I let the mayor's call go to voicemail and then instantly pressed play to listen to it.

"You know," he began, "that people from France can only stay in San Francisco for a total of three days without a special visa issued by the mayor's office. In case you haven't heard of this law, I just passed it this morning. And no, there will not be any visas issued until the next century."

I nearly laughed.

He was persistent as fuck. I'd give him that. He was not put off by the thought that I was basically sleeping with another man. He still wanted me. It was slightly insane.

Ryder watched me as I listened to this message.

He was naked. In my kitchen. Cooking for me.

Looking at him made me smile. His body was perfect.

"At least put an apron on," I said as he sautéed pancetta in olive oil, making it sizzle. "I don't want any part of your body burned."

He laughed. "I cook naked all the time."

I just shook my head.

"That call?" he said. "You look concerned. Your forehead crinkled."

"Oh," I said, thinking that I needed to work on my poker face. "It was the mayor."

"And?" Ryder said, plucking a small piece of cheese off a plate and putting it in his mouth.

"He wants to see me as soon as you leave town."

"And will you?" he asked, turning toward the refrigerator. "See him?"

I waited for a beat and then said, "Would you care?"

He turned back around. "I leave Monday," he said.

I closed my eyes. He'd avoided telling me that he had a plan. My stomach suddenly flip flopped.

"So soon?"

"I was going to tell you tonight," he said.

"You didn't answer my question," I said, leaning my chin onto my fist.

He didn't look at me. He slid the pancetta pasta into two pasta bowls and set them on the table.

"Would you care?" I said again in a soft voice from my spot on the couch.

He walked over, pulled me up, and grabbed my head, kissing me long and hard, his hands tangled in my hair.

"What do you think?" he said in a husky voice as he pulled back.

I stared at him.

"Come with me to France."

"Stay here," I said at nearly the same time.

We both gave strangled laughs.

"You can be a kept man. You don't need to work anymore."

He rolled his eyes and shook his head, but he was smiling.

"Gia, my life is half a world away. Your life is here. Me and you? It is ... impossible ..."

I pulled away. His words hurt more than I'd expected. Walking toward the bedroom I didn't look at him as I spoke.

"I think you need to change your flight and leave tomorrow," I said, trying to keep my voice neutral. "I don't want this to be any harder than it already is." I paused but he didn't say anything so I continued into the bedroom. "I'm staying at Darling's tonight. I'm going to take a shower, pack and then leave. You can stay here tonight."

It hurt but I knew it would hurt more if he stayed another five days. I had to make a clean break right then.

When I got out of the shower, he was gone.

The kitchen was cleaned up. The food was neatly put away under plastic wrap in the refrigerator.

A note on the counter. "Farewell my love."

I wouldn't be packing anything.

Instead I curled up on the couch and stared out the window at my city.

Are you loving *Deadly Justice*? Scan the QR code below to order your copy today!

ALSO BY KRISTI BELCAMINO

Enjoying Kristi Belcamino? Scan the code below to see her Amazon Author page!

Gia Santella Crime Thriller Series

Vendetta

Vigilante

Vengeance

Black Widow

Day of the Dead

Border Line

Night Fall

Stone Cold

Cold as Death

Cold Blooded

Dark Shadows

Dark Vengeance

Dark Justice

Deadly Justice

Deadly Lies

Additional books in series:

Taste of Vengeance

Lone Raven

Vigilante Crime Series

Blood & Roses

Blood & Fire

Blood & Bone

Blood & Tears

Queen of Spades Thrillers

Queen of Spades

The One-Eyed Jack

The Suicide King

The Ace of Clubs

The Joker

The Wild Card

High Stakes

Poker Face

Standalone Novels

Coming For You

Sanctuary City

The Girl in the River

Buried Secrets

Dead Wrong (Young Adult Mystery)

Gabriella Giovanni Mystery Series

Blessed are the Dead

Blessed are the Meek

Blessed are Those Who Weep

Blessed are Those Who Mourn

Blessed are the Peacemakers

Blessed are the Merciful

Nonfiction

Letters from a Serial Killer

ALSO BY WITHOUT WARRANT

More Thriller Series from Without Warrant Authors

Dana Gray Mysteries by C.J. Cross

Girl Left Behind

Girl on the Hill

Girl in the Grave

The Kenzie Gilmore Series by Biba Pearce

Afterburn

Dead Heat

Heatwave

Burnout

Deep Heat

Fever Pitch

Storm Surge (Coming Soon)

Willow Grace FBI Thrillers by Anya Mora

Shadow of Grace

Condition of Grace (Coming Soon)

Gia Santella Crime Thriller Series by Kristi Belcamino

Vendetta

Vigilante

Vengeance

Black Widow

Day of the Dead

Border Line

Night Fall

Stone Cold

Cold as Death

Cold Blooded

Dark Shadows

Dark Vengeance

Dark Justice

Deadly Justice

Deadly Lies

Vigilante Crime Series by Kristi Belcamino

Blood & Roses

Blood & Fire

Blood & Bone

Blood & Tears

Queen of Spades Thrillers by Kristi Belcamino

Queen of Spades

The One-Eyed Jack

The Suicide King

The Ace of Clubs

The Joker

The Wild Card

High Stakes

Poker Face

AUTHOR'S NOTE

When I was 16, I read Jackie Collins' book, *Lucky*, and it rocked my world. For the first time in my prolific reading life (yes, I was the kid holed up in my room reading as many books as I could as often as I could), I met a character who was not only Italian-American like me, but a strong, powerful, and successful badass woman who didn't take crap from anybody and loved to have sex!

Although I had dreamed of being a writer, it never seemed like a realistic dream and my attempts at writing seemed pitiful. So I studied journalism and became a reporter—it was a way to be a writer and have a steady paycheck.

It was only when I was in my forties that I got the guts to write a book. And it was a few years after that I was brave enough to write the character I really wanted to write—Gia Santella.

She's not Lucky Santangelo, of course. I mean, nobody could be as cool as Lucky is, but I like to think that maybe Gia and Lucky would have been friends.

Gia is my alter ego. The woman who does and says things I

never could or would, but whom I admire and would love to be friends with.

If you like her, I'm pretty sure we'd be the best of friends in real life!

x Kristi

ABOUT THE AUTHOR

Kristi Belcamino is a USA Today bestseller, an Agatha, Anthony, Barry & Macavity finalist, and an Italian Mama who bakes a tasty biscotti.

Her books feature strong, kickass, independent women facing unspeakable evil in order to seek justice for those unable to do so themselves.

In her former life, as an award-winning crime reporter at newspapers in California, she flew over Big Sur in an FA-18 jet with the Blue Angels, raced a Dodge Viper at Laguna Seca, attended barbecues at the morgue, and conversed with serial killers.

During her decade covering crime, Belcamino wrote and reported about many high-profile cases including the Laci Peterson murder and Chandra Levy disappearance. She has appeared on *Inside Edition* and local television shows. She now writes fiction and works part-time as a reporter covering the police beat for the St. Paul *Pioneer Press*.

Her work has appeared in such prominent publications as *Salon*, the *Miami Herald*, *San Jose Mercury News,* and *Chicago Tribune*.

- facebook.com/kristibelcaminowriter
- instagram.com/kristibelcaminobooks
- tiktok.com/@kristibelcaminobooks

Printed in the USA
CPSIA information can be obtained
at www.ICGtesting.com
LVHW020000171223
766691LV00051B/1622